She'd leave Slocum his saddlebags. She couldn't very well take them—he was using them for a pillow. All she was taking was the horse and the saddle and one of the canteens. And the Winchester.

She turned toward the rock where she'd carefully leaned it. It wasn't there.

From behind her, the sound of a cocking rifle broke the stillness.

She wheeled round to find Slocum slouched casually against a tall boulder, the Winchester in one hand, butted against his stomach. It was pointed straight at her.

With his free hand, he thumbed back his hat. "You looking for this?"

JAKE LOGAN

SLOCUM AND
THE IRISH LASS

JOVE BOOKS, NEW YORK

SLOCUM AND THE IRISH LASS

A Jove Book / published by arrangement with
the author

PRINTING HISTORY
Jove edition / September 1997

The Putnam Berkley World Wide Web site address is
http://www.berkley.com

ISBN: 0-515-12155-X

A JOVE BOOK®
Jove Books are published by The Berkley Publishing Group,
200 Madison Avenue, New York, New York 10016.
JOVE and the "J" design are trademarks
belonging to Jove Publications, Inc.

PRINTED IN THE UNITED STATES OF AMERICA

10 9 8 7 6 5 4 3 2 1

SLOCUM AND
THE IRISH LASS

1

The woman stood, alone and swaying slightly, on the crest of a hill.

Her face was covered in a thin layer of dried mud. Her skirts were ragged and torn, and her hair hung in matted strings from her head. Dried blood stained and stiffened the fabric of her sleeves and bodice. Her parched lips were peeling, and would soon begin to crack. Shading bleary eyes with a hand that was almost too heavy to lift, she searched the sun-blasted distance for any signs of life.

Nothing. Nothing for miles.

She hardly noticed when her legs gave out and she dropped to her knees. She wavered there for a second, her vision swirling dimly.

Was there movement out on the plain? A tiny shimmering speck lost in the heat waves, now visible, now lost again. It could have been white or Apache, could have been a cow or a horse, even a leftover army camel. Or nothing.

Her mouth moved, a hoarse and brittle whisper escaping it.

"Daddy?"

Then she fell forward, facedown, on the gravelly desert.

Two more days and he'd be in Yuma.

If he didn't get jumped by renegade Apaches, if Mexican bandits didn't take a liking to his horse, if some idiot with more buckshot than brains didn't ambush him, if his horse didn't step in a prairie dog hole . . .

If, if, if. He decided he had much too much time on his hands.

Slocum had been through this desolate stretch of Arizona before, ridden through it—fought his way through it, more like—during the Apache Wars, back when he was scouting for the army. But there'd been a lot of water under the bridge since then. Wyoming, Montana, Texas, Oregon, you name it; fighting the Cheyenne, fighting over women, fighting greedy men and freezing winters and blast-furnace summers . . . a lot of water, and very little of it potable.

He'd just come from whiling away a few weeks in the arms of a handsome little gal in New Mexico Territory. Victoria was her name, and she had hair the color of fresh-churned butter, and the smooth disposition—and smooth pale body—to match.

But finally, his wandering ways had taken over, and now he found himself in the middle of the godforsaken Arizona desert, and wishing he'd just stayed put in New Mexico. For a change.

He passed over a disturbance in the desert floor, and warily reined in his horse. A heavy wagon pulled by a team of four horses and accompanied by four riders, maybe five, had passed this way recently. They were headed south. Odd that they'd be clear out here, far from any road. Then again, not so odd. He was getting jumpy, that was all. There weren't many roads in Arizona, and miners had to go to town for supplies too.

He pulled out his canteen and took a swig. He'd feel better after he got to Yuma. He always felt better after he passed a night at Sarah Bowman's. They called her the Great Western, all red hair and blue eyes and six feet tall. And even if the Great Western was a good bit over the hill these days, she always had the prettiest *señoritas* north of the border working at her place.

He capped the canteen, then wiped his mouth on his sleeve. That was the ticket: a wild night with a sloe-eyed *señorita*, then a good confab with the Great Western before he moved on. She had a story for every occasion, and most of them were humdingers too. Then maybe another night with the *señorita*. Maybe Consuelo, if she was still at the Great Western's.

Two years ago, when he'd stopped by, bound for Tombstone, she'd settled on his lap before he'd sat all the way down in the Great Western's parlor.

"This one is mine," she'd said with a slow, sly grin, picking up his hand and placing it over her breast. "Isn't he, my handsome gringo?" And then she'd led him to her room.

Mirrors, hundreds of them, from palm-sized fragments to picture-sized to tiny chips and shards, decorated the windowless walls like a shimmering mosaic. He'd seen himself reflected in the light of a thousand reflected candles. A thousand John Slocums, all with their britches down, all with swollen pricks. And a thousand Consuelos: naked, her lush, brown breasts rubbing beaded nipples along the fur of his thighs as she went down on her knees before him.

She had licked the purple head of his cock once, swirling her tongue lazily around the head. *"Muy bueno,"* she'd purred, as one hand stroked his ass and the other curled around the base of his shaft, her fingers not quite meeting. *"Muy grande.* You watch the mirrors, señor," she'd said with a sultry wink, "and you might see the God." And then she'd slowly taken him inside her hot, wet mouth and suckled him like a sleepy calf on its mama's teat.

He'd "seen the God" three times before morning, and once more after the cock's crow, and that one-night layover in Yuma had turned into three.

He was about to tap the stud with his spurs when a bit of movement to the north caught his eye. Immediately he tensed. Apaches? The days of Geronimo were over since General Miles had locked him up, and most of his people were corralled in that stinking hellhole at San Carlos. But stragglers were squirreled away down in Mexico, and sometimes forayed north of the border. They were more than happy to take out their torment on any hapless white man they could get their hands on.

He'd seen too many men skinned alive or with their brains boiled out over slow fires. He had no desire whatsoever to participate.

He pulled his scope free and focused on the top of the hill, where he'd seen the flutter of movement. Something blue. The wind lifted it again, snapped it. Blue gingham?

He collapsed the brass spyglass, stuck it back in his pack, and nudged the stud forward. He'd have a little look-see at the other side of the hill before he went galloping up there, big as you please.

She came awake not with a sputter, but with a shout, and swung her fist as hard as she could into the dark shape crouched over her.

The man, taken by surprise, toppled back on his butt even as he went for his cross-draw holster.

She'd never seen anybody pull a gun so fast—the Colt was out before his backside hit the ground—and she thought, *Jesus, Mary, and Joseph!* while she croaked, "Don't shoot!" with what was left of her voice.

He didn't put the gun down, much to her chagrin. Instead, he stared at her, his free hand coming up to rub at his jaw where her fist had found purchase, and stared down the barrel at her. It was disconcerting, to say the least.

"You're welcome," he said at last, scowling. The gun slid away, into its holster.

"W-what?" she rasped. He had green eyes. Green eyes for Irish luck, and she was in desperate need of some luck right now. Please, let him be a nice man! Or at least a greedy one.

He was still scowling, though. "I said, you're welcome. Though I've had thank-yous that were a helluva lot nicer."

He got back to his knees and bent over her. He held a canteen to her lips, and she drank gratefully, the warm water coursing down her throat, spilling out over her chin.

"I'd work on my manners if I were you, lady," he said, then took the canteen away, long before she was close to sated.

She fought him for it, although she'd exhausted her reserves trying to knock him out, so her fight was little more than a halfhearted tug.

"Don't be greedy," he said curtly, and stoppered the canteen. "Everybody for five miles can see us. I'm going to get you down off this hill first. You can have more water while I decide what to do with you."

He lifted her up in his arms—*strong arms*, she thought without meaning to, *broad chest*—and carried her toward his horse. She hadn't seen the horse before. It was a stallion, heavy-muscled and bright copper-bay, and its rump was blanketed in white with big coppery spots.

An appaloosa. Frank used to ride an appaloosa.

She turned her head away, tucking it into the man's shoulder, trying to remember Frank's face.

Her head didn't stay tucked for long, though. He boosted her into the saddle, then swung up behind her. He fumbled under his leg—in his saddlebags, she thought—and after a moment handed her a chip of salt, saying, "Suck on that."

It was dirty, but she brushed it off as best she could and put it in her mouth. Immediately he pulled her tight against his torso. It was like being in a flesh-and-blood corset.

"You have a name?" he asked as he gathered his reins and headed the stud carefully down the slope.

She had to think for a moment. "Maddie," she whispered finally, through a ragged throat, around the salt that didn't do anything to slake her thirst. "Maddie O'Hara."

She wanted Daddy Jim. She wanted Frank.

She wanted to be back home, churning butter and mending tack and baking up vanilla pecan cakes and crown roasts and blueberry waffles to sate Daddy Jim's massive epicurean appetite. And complaining that in the two whole years she'd been there, nothing had ever happened.

But something had most certainly happened, and now Frank was dead, and Daddy Jim was God knows where. She looked like something the cat had dragged in and felt worse, she was sucking on dirty salt, and worst of all, she was at the mercy of this man, this nameless man who wore more guns than the Seventh Cavalry.

Two Colts set in a cross-draw rig and a Winchester in the saddle scabbard. Those, she'd seen. He probably had a pistol in his left boot, an Arkansas toothpick in the right, and a blade in his lapel. Likely a sawed-off shotgun up one sleeve and a hideout derringer up the other.

And another gun in his hat too.

And he looked mean, like he could use that arsenal. Like he *had* used it. Why, he could take her to his camp and have at her—have at her repeatedly!—and there wouldn't be a thing she could do about it. He'd probably subject her to all sorts of indignities. Make her walk around the camp naked, or bend her over a rock whenever he got the urge, or . . .

She had a sudden urge to pat her hair and straighten her bodice, but resisted.

Why, it could take weeks before he finished with her! Of course, then he'd probably have the bad taste to kill her, and no one would ever be the wiser. They'd think she'd been carried off in the wagon, along with Daddy Jim.

No one would ever suspect that she'd been picked up by some out-of-work cowboy who was really an over-armed maniac rapist in dire need of a shave. No one would find her corpse, left naked in the middle of nowhere for the vultures to pick clean.

But, she thought, brightening, maybe he wasn't a maniac or a killer. Maybe he was just sex-crazed. And then she thought that she had more important things to worry about. Sex was the last thing she should be thinking about.

The sun had fried her brain, that was all. He was more likely a killer than a rapist, more likely a dumb saddle tramp than either of those.

But still . . . A dumb sex-crazed maniac killer.

Fine, just fine. Out of the frying pan and into the volcano.

"By the way," came the rumbling voice close behind her, "my name's Slocum. John Slocum."

"Hullo," she said meekly. Did murderers

give you their names? Never having met one, she didn't know.

No, they probably didn't. They probably made up a name. John Slocum sounded pretty made-up, didn't it?

She said, "That real, or a summer name?" and immediately thought better of it. She needed more water. She had to start thinking straight. Words were pouring out of her mouth—and ideas coming into her head—of their own accord.

The man behind her tightened his grip around her rib cage, crushing her back against his chest as the appaloosa skidded down a steep patch. And as the wind went out of her, she thought, *He's not even going to make me walk around naked first, he's just going to crush me to death!*

But he said, "Slocum's from my papa." The appaloosa quite handily threaded its way between two yuccas, then made a little hop down to better footing. "My mother picked John. Anything else you're burning to know?"

She pounded on his restraining arm, and when he loosened it, took a huge gulp of air, swallowing the salt in the process. "If you're going to squash the wind out of me, you could at least do it face-to-face!" she blurted out, ending in a dry-throated croak.

There was a silence—oh, she wished she

could see his face! Then again, maybe she didn't.

All he said—after a time—was, "I'll keep it in mind."

2

Slocum shook his head.

Five sentences out of the girl on the way down the hill, and most all of them cranky, and then she hadn't said another word all the way to this feeble excuse for a spring. She was beside it now, kneeling a few feet away, her back to him, washing her hair. A fat lot of good it would do her. One good blowup from the southeast, and she'd be combing grit and burrs out of it for days.

He liked what he saw, though. Brunette, almost black hair. Blue eyes beneath delicately arched brows. Her face was pretty, or at least, he thought it was. It looked like she'd rubbed mud on her face to keep the sun from her skin, and it was hard to tell what was under all that dirt. He wouldn't know now until she turned around. Probably to glare at him.

"I don't suppose you'd have any soap," she'd said after she'd drunk her fill, as if she didn't expect a creature as dull as he was to know soap from a goat turd.

He'd been so startled—and annoyed—by the question (and the way she'd asked it) that he'd pulled out the cake and shoved it at her. And now she was washing her goddamn hair. At least she had the brains to do it over the ground and not the water, where she'd foul the spring.

Well, the rear view was a nice one. He'd settle for that, for the time being. A nice round fanny—not too big, not too small, just the right size to keep a pair of hands busy—was graphically outlined by the torn skirts snugged over it.

He watched as, still kneeling, she poured a cup of water over her head, then another, the soap whisking down, soaking quickly into the parched earth. The line of her neck reminded him of a swan.

He wondered if she had anything to do with the wagon tracks he'd seen. If Little Miss Sunshine's attitude was any indicator, they'd probably thrown her off and said "good riddance."

Grunting, he turned to one side and stared out into the hills again. It would be dark in an hour, an hour he intended to spend riding toward Yuma.

He planned to avoid the sand-dune desert. Go across to the river, then south along its banks. It would cost him some time, but then, he wasn't in a hurry. Well, he was in a hurry to get to the Great Western's place, and Consuelo, that was for sure. But not in so much of a hurry that he'd take a chance on dying for it.

Practiced eyes searched the horizon for the smallest thing out of order, and found none. He made another quarter turn.

Behind him, he heard splashing. What was she doing over there, swimming? He called, "You about finished?"

"Hold your horses," came the reply. Still cranky.

Slocum sighed. If he had to pick up a woman out here, why couldn't she have been in a friendlier frame of mind?

He hadn't asked her about the blood on her dress, and she hadn't told him. It had been the first thing he checked when he found her on the hill, but he hadn't found a bullet hole or a knife's gash, just lots of dried blood. It had soaked clear through to the skin too. Considering her current state of mind, he didn't figure it would be a good idea to tell her how he'd found that out.

Pretty breasts, though, at least the one he'd seen. Round and high and white, and capped with a pale brownish pink. A shame she was keeping them all to herself.

"Finished." The voice came from behind him—right behind him—and he spun, the Peacemaker drawn on reflex, only to jam it back in the holster when he remembered himself.

He growled, "Stop sneaking. I could have shot you."

She frowned. "I can't help it if I walk softly." She shoved the soap at him. "You know, you're awfully jumpy. I think you've been out on the desert too long. And you could use a shave." Then she turned her back and marched to the spring to wash the last of the soap off her hands.

He watched her walk away, barely aware of the soap dripping in his hand, spattering his boots.

She was downright gorgeous.

After an hour's ride—during which she found her senses at last and decided that Slocum was neither a murderer or a rapist, even if he was on the surly side—Slocum stopped the horse in a sheltered spot, and proceeded to set up camp.

He settled his horse in first. That was a good sign. You could tell a great deal about a man by the way he treated his horse.

And he was fast with that cross-draw gun. Fast? Lightning described it better. She shivered again, thinking about how quickly that Colt had appeared. Yes, he certainly had the arsenal for what she had in mind, and if he was half as good with the rifle as he was with that Colt . . .

"Where are you taking me?" she said, rather abruptly.

He looked up from the small fire he was building, then turned his attention back to it. He didn't seem to look at a person for more than a second.

"West to the river. Then down to Yuma," he said.

"Oro Tiempo's closer. We could be there tomorrow."

He fed a stick into the fire. "Not going south. Yet."

He was not only sullen, he was pigheaded. She lifted her chin and said, "I'll pay you."

He looked up from the fire, his expression sullen. "I said I'm going west. Can you cook?"

Of all the mean sonofabitching sidewinders! He hadn't even looked at her crosswise—let alone made her take off her clothes, which she'd actually been looking forward to, in a perverse sort of way—but now he was being just plain rude. She crossed her arms and stuck her nose in the air, scowling. "I only cook snakes. Like you."

"Then you're in luck," he said, and pulling a knife from nowhere, hurled it at her.

She screamed and dived to one side just as the blade dug into the ground.

And severed the head of a rattler, not three feet from where she'd stood. The headless body flopped and writhed, the tail rattling a halfhearted and useless warning.

He came around the fire and put his hand down. She thought he was going to help her

up and reached for it, but at the last minute
he changed direction and retrieved the knife,
which he carefully wiped on his britches and
stuck back in his boot sheath. So that's where
it had come from! Then he picked up the still-
coiling diamondback and tossed it down in
front of her.

"Start cooking," he said.

She looked at the snake, which was making
its last few feeble flops. She looked up at him.
Two could play at this game. "Fine," she said.
"And might I ask for the loan of your cutlery,
Mr. Slocum?"

Without expression, he handed her the
knife. She got up, taking the snake with her—
thank God it had stopped moving—and
moved closer to the fire. One deft slice, a quick
chop, and a good yank later, she threw the
skin at his feet and stood defiantly, the long,
pink, wet carcass swinging from her hand.

She said, "Stewed, roasted, or medallions?"

Well, she could cook, he'd say that for her. He
took another bite of stew and chewed thoughtfully. She was across the fire, sitting sideways
to him, her attention on her dinner. He had
his first good chance to study her since she'd
regained consciousness.

She was tallish, but not too tall—about five
feet six, he reckoned, for her head had just
reached his shoulder—and delicate in build.
Not scrawny, though, just fine-boned. No, not

scrawny, not by a long shot. The tiny waist he'd put his arm around when he'd mounted up had been supple, and there was some meat on the ribs. The back that had dug into his chest hadn't been bony either. Just . . . nice.

His cock stirred, and he shifted, clearing his throat.

She turned her face toward him. "Did you say something?"

"Good stew," he mumbled, and ate, staring at his plate.

"Oh." She frowned slightly, then turned away again.

He didn't know what the hell was wrong with him. The Lord knows, he could handle a woman. Any woman, any time. How had this little slip of nothing, dressed in rags, managed to cow him?

And another thing: Where had she come from? Any other woman in similar circumstances would have spilled the story, and likely more of it than he wanted to hear, within the first two minutes of consciousness. But not her. Not old close-lipped what's-her-name. What *was* her name? Maddie. That was it, Maddie O'Hara.

And just what was her story anyhow? Well, he wasn't going to ask her. He'd be damned if he'd ask her. She could just keep it to herself.

He stabbed another chunk of snake meat, picking up some onion with it. His last onion.

He pushed it in his mouth, chewing angrily, watching her again.

How could she just sit there, so prim and desirable despite that bloody rag of a dress, nibbling on her stew and staring out into the darkness at nothing? And what did she want to go to Oro Tiempo for? It was nothing but a mining town in the goddamn middle of nowhere.

She'd go to Yuma and like it. And once they got there, she'd be on her own. There were plenty of other women in Yuma, women who actually liked him. Consuelo, for instance.

He was thinking about those mirrored walls again, when suddenly the girl turned toward him, taking him by surprise. "Mr. Slocum," she said, her plate balanced on her knees, "is there nothing that will turn you toward Oro Tiempo?"

He could think of a thing or three, but he doubted she was offering. She'd tied her hair, now dry, back into a dark horsetail that poured halfway down her back. Her skin was white as milk, and the dark point of a widow's peak combined with a slightly pointed chin to give her face a heart-shaped look. Even in the dim firelight, he caught an occasional glimpse of the blue of her eyes.

When he didn't answer, her lush lips parted to say, "You're staring, Mr. Slocum. I must get a horse. I have to go south."

A woman traveling alone out here was a

woman on the verge of suicide. He thought of all the things that might happen to her, and then he thought she probably deserved every single one of them, if this was how she acted. She had to be twenty-four, maybe twenty-five, and she was a real beauty, yet she wore no wedding ring. The way he figured it, she was one of those perpetual virgins who scared off all comers with a smart mouth, and ended up a skinny, dried-up old maid, smacking people with her cane.

Against his better judgment, he said, "Why south?"

"Because that's where they went," she said impatiently, with an air that suggested she'd never heard such a stupid question. "Because that's where they took him. I trailed them as far as I could, and now you've got me all off course with your meddling!"

He filled his cheeks with air, then blew it out. Who were "they," and why did they take "him," and who the hell was "him" anyway?

He supposed he could ask.

He supposed he could just shoot her and be done with it.

But instead, he swept his hat from his head and held it out to the side. "Well, pardon me, ma'am. If I'd known you were doggin' a trail, I would've just let you be."

The hat went back on his head, and he stabbed another bite of stew, a good deal more forcefully than need be, and stuffed it in his mouth.

"You needn't be impertinent," she sniffed. "I said I'd pay you."

Slocum ignored her. "Course, right about now you'd be buzzard bait," he continued around a mouthful of food. "Or dinner for some lonely coyote. Or playing squaw to eight or ten wormy Apaches. But far be it from me to interfere with a lady's plans. See, I don't need your money. I'm going to Yuma, and my horse is going to Yuma with me. You can come with us or not. Up to you."

Abruptly, she stood up. Her plate clattered to the rocky soil, splattering her ragged skirts with stew. "Honestly! If you aren't the most exasperating, the most annoying, the most infuriating, the most . . . the most . . ."

She ran out of words, and sent him a glare that would have turned a lesser man into a pool of whimpering mush. Then she turned her back on him, arms crossed.

For the first time, Slocum smiled. "Yes, ma'am," he said softly, as he poured himself a cup of coffee. "Reckon I am."

3

The sonofabitch! Maddie thought, as she tried to lift the saddle without making any noise. *The lousy, stinking sonofabitch!*

The leather creaked and she froze, her stare focused on Slocum. He twitched a little in his sleep, and then his breathing pattern resumed. Deep and slow. Good.

She brought the saddle up to her chest and turned toward the horse, considering how in the world she'd ever boost it up there without making a sound.

The stud eyed her sleepily. Under her breath, she whispered, "Don't move, you spotted pot of mucilage," heaved the saddle up onto the horse's back, and immediately looked to see if Slocum had moved.

He hadn't. He was still sound asleep with his hat over his face and his arms crossed over his chest. She allowed herself a small sigh of relief, then got back to business. She rocked the saddle back into place, then went to the off side to let down the stirrup and girth as quietly as possible.

The horse was a good one, fifteen-two if she

didn't miss her guess, and with lots of bottom to go all day. Her weight would mean nothing to a horse like this. Once she got clear of Slocum she'd be able to find those skunks in no time at all. She'd invested too much time—and emotion—in Daddy Jim to see him snatched away from her by a band of cutthroats.

Maybe she didn't always agree with him about what was best, but she loved him and he loved her, and she supposed that was what counted. Hadn't he come all the way to Chicago to find her? Hadn't he broken the doctor's bad news to her and held her hand? Hadn't he brought her to the ranch and treated her like his own kin?

Maybe a little too much like his own kin. There was that thing with Frank. She was still a puzzled by that. Why would Daddy Jim marry her off to a man she hardly knew, a man she'd only met once, a year ago? Why, they were practically strangers. She hadn't even slept with him!

She tiptoed around, back to the horse's near side, and reached under his belly for the girth. Well, Daddy Jim had brought her down from Chicago, and she owed him. She would have died of the consumption if not for him. She owed him her life. She also owed him a distinct drop in her income.

But then, what was a little thing like that compared to coughing up blood and keeling over? And she'd learned a new trade on account of his exotic tastes. She supposed if worse came to worst, she could always be a chef.

She kneed the horse in his belly, and quickly took up the slack in the latigo. None of it mattered now anyway. Frank was dead, so that sort of canceled out the engagement, to say nothing of the marriage. And Daddy Jim had gone south, in the wagon with the gold.

They'd thought she was dead, she supposed. When the shooting had started and one of the guards, Sanchez, had fallen on her, she'd screamed. And then something had hit her on the head, or maybe she'd fallen on something, and that was the last thing she remembered. All that blood—Sanchez's blood—had saved her life. Too bad it had ended Sanchez's. She'd liked him.

Satisfied that the girth was snug enough, she dropped the stirrup down into place. The leathers were far too long, but she'd worry about that later, after she got a safe distance from the man. How tall was he, anyway? Six one? Six two? And the boots he wore made him even taller.

She leaned her head on the stirrup leather. Why were the attractive ones always so pigheaded or mean or stupid or all three?

Well, not all the attractive ones. Max Slade was a helluva a guy, big and tall and good-looking. He always booked her for a solid three days when he came to Chicago on business, and tipped her an extra hundred in double eagles to boot. Of course, the place he put her tip was a little bizarre ("Your Max is leavin' now, darling, so spread them pretty legs wide . . ."), but it was well worth it.

Roy Schwartz was nice, and good-looking too. Once he'd brought her an ostrich-plume hat, all the way from New York City. And Hiram Johnson was six feet six in his stocking feet. Almost as pretty as a woman, and gentle as a lamb. Always took off his hat, although never his socks.

No, all the attractive men weren't pigheaded or stupid or mean. Just this one.

Careless of her to find him so appealing. Any other time, any other place . . . It had been a long time since she'd had a good man in her arms, in her bed. And Slocum looked to be— No. Daddy Jim came first. Anything extra would just complicate matters.

And so she was settling the dilemma for good. She'd leave Slocum his saddlebags. She couldn't very well take them—he was using them for a pillow. All she was taking was the horse and saddle and one of the canteens. And the Winchester.

She turned toward the rock where she'd carefully leaned it. It wasn't there.

From behind her, the sound of a cocking rifle broke the stillness.

She wheeled round to find Slocum slouched casually against a tall boulder, the Winchester in one hand, butted against his stomach. It was pointed straight at her.

With his free hand, he thumbed back his hat. "You looking for this?"

She didn't even have the good grace to look ashamed, he thought. She just stared at him, her gaze level.

"Well?" she demanded at last. "Aren't you going to shoot me?" Her foot tapped three times, impatiently.

"Reckon I ought to," he drawled, letting no expression cross his face. "Third time being the charm, and all. And as I recall, this is the third time today I've been called on to point a firearm at you. You know, you draw 'em enough times without shootin' 'em, and they get lazy. Won't hit a damn thing."

He watched her face for any trace of a smile, but didn't see one, so he didn't smile either. "But before I put a nice neat hole between your . . . in your chest, that is," he went on, "why don't you slide that saddle off old Pete, real easy, and then why don't you sit down on that rock over there. Then you can tell me why the hell you're in such an all-fired hurry to kite out on your own. On my horse."

He indicated the Winchester with a slight nod of his head. "You know, this here's a beautiful weapon and it can do a lot of things, but it can't make its own ammunition. You should have taken a box."

This time he got the stamp of her foot for his trouble. But she stripped the tack off the appy, dropping it to the ground with a thud, and then plopped her pretty fanny on the rock.

"Where do you want me to start?" Even the question had the ring of an accusation.

He lowered the Winchester and sat down, an ankle cocked over his knee. "Anywhere you want."

He got the story, more or less. It seemed that she and her daddy had a place up by Three Wives. It seemed she also had a fiancé by the name of Frank—that took him by surprise, for he was amazed that anyone could stand to be around her long enough to get engaged—and Frank was away most of the time on business. She didn't say what the business was, and he didn't ask.

This ranch of her daddy's turned out to be sitting on top of a fairly large gold deposit that spat nuggets down into the river to beat the band, and he'd put ranching aside in favor of nursing his gold fever. He'd set out with a wagon load of dust and nuggets and three guards, on his way to the smelter down at Caballo Loco, and she'd come along, seeing as Daddy was to drop her in Halcyon along the way. There Frank would meet her, and wait for Daddy's return.

Except that when they got to Halcyon, they learned that good old Frank had been killed by a runaway horse up north somewhere. Slocum didn't see that the girl was all that broken up about it, but made no comment.

The troupe went on toward Caballo Loco, but halfway there they were waylaid by highwaymen. About five of them, the girl said. The guards were killed and she was left for dead—which explained the blood on her dress—but the gold and the wagon were gone, and so was her daddy.

The story was so full of holes that he could have swung a dead cat in it, then driven through a team of mules.

But he said, "How much gold?"

"About fifteen thousand," she said, as if the amount were neither here nor there. And then her expression changed suddenly from flat to imploring. "Please, Mr. Slocum. Please help me find my daddy? I've got some money. Here, I'll pay you."

She scrambled with her skirts, and he got a quick, moonlit glimpse of slender calf and creamy thigh before the fabric covered them again.

She held out the greenbacks, a fat roll of them. "See? That's almost two hundred dollars. More than a cowhand makes in six months. It's yours, all yours. Just help me find my daddy."

And then, much to his surprise, she started to cry, her hands covering her face. The roll of bills dropped to the dust at her feet.

He was almost taken in by it. He almost felt bad, almost got up and went to comfort her, until he saw her sneak a peek at him through her fingers.

He heaved a sigh. "All right," he said. Immediately the girl looked up. He'd been right. Not a trace of a tear caught the moonlight.

"All right, what?" she said.

"All right, we'll turn around and go back to where I found you, and follow the tracks. But you can keep your money."

She snatched it up. Her brows furrowed. "What?"

"Got no use for scrip. If we find your daddy—dead or alive—and if we find this gold wagon, I'll take a cut. Say, ten percent?"

She jumped to her feet. "Are you crazy? That's fifteen hundred dollars! You couldn't make that much in your miserable, saddle-tramping life! And furthermore, I know Daddy Jim's alive. I feel it in my bones. So I don't want to hear anymore of that 'dead or alive' business. Four hundred in gold."

"Fifteen."

The girl stiffened. "Five."

"Fifteen."

"Mr. Slocum, you are impossible. Seven."

He pulled his hat low on his forehead, and leaned back, rifle across his knees. He was enjoying this. He said, "Fifteen."

She pulled in air through her teeth angrily.

Pretty teeth, white and even. "One thousand. And that's my final offer."

He slowly got to his feet and stretched. "I think you'll like Yuma."

He sauntered back to his bedroll and eased himself down, the rifle at his side. He pulled his hat over his face, leaving enough room so that he could see beneath the brim, sideways, in case she decided to take a rock to his skull.

Silently, he began to count.

He was up to forty-seven when she said, "Oh, all right! Fifteen hundred. But we leave now."

Slocum was glad the hat covered his grin. "We leave in the morning. Trust me, honey, those boys ain't movin' right now either, and we can make a lot better time on old Pete than they can with that wagon."

He watched as her hands balled into fists at her sides. She brought them up, shaking them stiffly at him as she let out a frustrated grunt. Then she walked to the other side of the fire, out of his sight. He heard the sounds of her settling in on her blanket.

He wondered what had gotten to her more—his refusal to travel at night, or that "honey."

Either way, it was a chancy situation he'd gotten himself into. At best. The girl's story didn't ring true. She was leaving out an important detail, or details, and that bothered him. Also, for somebody who'd just lost her fiancé, had her daddy kidnapped, lost fifteen thousand in gold with dead bodies bleeding all over her, and had just about walked herself to death on the Arizona desert, she seemed just a little too casual.

He picked up his hat, just slightly, and looked at her. Asleep.

Well, he'd figure it out later. Yuma and Consuelo could wait a day or two. And there might be fifteen hundred in it for him.

4

"But I don't want to stop!" Behind him, Maddie pounded a fist on his back.

"Get down."

She beat on his shoulders with hard little knuckles. "I insist you get this horse going this *instant!*"

Slocum set his mouth into a line. The whole morning had been one long argument, and if she'd been riding in front, he would have simply hauled off and slugged her. "Get down. Old Pete's tired and he needs water."

"No! I *insist* that you keep on going."

Gritting his teeth, he muttered, "You asked for it, honey." Abruptly, he stood in the stirrups and swung his right leg back to dismount—and swept her off the horse in the process.

His boot hit the ground a half second after her backside did.

"You fiend!" she snarled up at him, more surprised than hurt, by the looks of it. "You idiot!" She stuck a hand beneath her, pulling free a rock and rubbing at her fanny. "You could have killed me!"

Slocum loosened the girth, then pulled down the canvas water bag.

"Live in hope," he said, without expression, and proceeded to water the stud. Old Pete closed his eyes and drank gratefully. At least somebody appreciated him.

They'd been trailing the wagon since dawn. About a half hour ago, they'd passed the spot where the men had made camp the night before. Before them, the desert stretched out like a hot blanket speckled with dusty greens and browns. Hell's patchwork quilt.

On the horizon, a string of distant hills shimmered in the heat. Los Cuervos, if he didn't miss his guess. The Crows. Low hills, then a warren of canyons that went right down to the border. He wanted to catch up with Daddy and the boys quick, in case they took it into their heads to duck into that maze. Right now the trail was jogging east, toward Caballo Loco and the smelter, but you never could tell.

"Well?" came the impatient voice from behind him. "Is he rested yet?"

Slocum didn't turn toward her. Pete had stopped drinking. A fly crawled up the horse's pastern, and it stamped a striped hoof lazily, then nudged Slocum with its speckled nose.

"I know, boy," Slocum said softly to the horse. "She's a goddamn tail-twister, isn't she?"

Then louder, so that the girl could hear him, he said, "Let's go."

She stomped over, rubbing at her fanny and obviously expecting him to mount up and put a hand down to her, but instead he fastened the water bag behind the cantle, took down the reins, and started walking.

She stood there a moment, and then he heard a crashing through the brittle brush as she ran to catch up with him. Nothing quiet about her today.

"Mr. Slocum! What are you doing?" she demanded, once she caught up.

"Giving Pete a breather. He's been carrying double for a long time."

She gave a little snort. "How long are we going to have to walk?"

He finally looked at her. When they'd broken camp that morning, he'd given her a blanket to drape over her head and shield her from the sun. But she'd let it slip, and her face was rosy with the beginnings of a sunburn. Without stopping, he reached over and grabbed the top of it, yanking it forward so that it shaded her face.

She lurched to the side and pulled the blanket around her like a shield. "Stop that, Mr. Slocum! I'll brook no familiarity."

Was there a hint of a dare in there somewhere? It was too hot to puzzle it out. And it must be six times hotter under that blanket. Good.

He kept walking and said, "Fine. Have it your way. Get sunburnt."

By then she'd recovered from the insult of being touched. She said, "Oh," and marched on without another word.

No "I'm sorry," or "excuse me," or even "oh, dear!" Not that he expected a whole lot of fine manners west of the Mississippi. Or even east of the Mississippi, come to think of it. But he might have expected at least one word of thanks for scraping her up off that hilltop yesterday.

Bitch.

She was walking about fifteen feet ahead now. She'd picked up the body of the blanket and looped it up over her shoulders, but the part that went over her head stayed where he'd put it, he noticed.

Her pretty little rump swished from side to side as she walked. Dark, damp patches stained the back of her bodice. He suspected the front was the same. The blanket was hot, but it was all he had to offer in the way of protection from the sun. And frankly, seeing her hot and uncomfortable was pleasant, in a vengeful sort of way.

He called, "You all right up there?"

She didn't answer, just straightened and gave a shake of her head—and her blanket shawl—and walked faster.

Fine with him. Just made her hips swish more.

He kept on walking that way, leading the stud and watching the girl in front of him in amused detachment, for ten minutes, fifteen, twenty. He finally decided he'd punished her enough, and was about to call to her to tell her they could mount up again, when she stopped.

Her knees buckled, and she crumpled.

He dropped the stud's reins and went to her. Her face was unnaturally red, and not from sunburn, he knew. Damn her anyway! He tried to think when she'd last asked him to pass the canteen. It must have been hours ago.

She hadn't quite gotten heat-stroked all the way, just enough to slow him down.

He whistled up Pete, and in the shade of the horse's body, poured water over her face, then held the canteen to her lips. This time when she came to, she didn't take a swing at him. She just lay limply in his arms, blinking slowly.

He offered the canteen again and she drank, then pushed his hand—and the canteen— away.

"I'm fine," she said. She was weak, but still full of defiance. "I'm just fine. Now let me up."

It came as something of a shock to Slocum that what he had the urge to do was kiss her. Kiss her and open the front of her dresss or maybe rip it off. Kiss her and suck on those sweet rosy nipples until they were twisted tight as corkscrews, then take her fast and hard, burying his cock to the hilt in her again and again.

Or maybe slow. He'd like to see her scream for more. Pound his shoulders and beg him.

"Slocum, I . . ." The girl paused, as if she'd read his expression and liked the idea. But then she scowled so quickly that he thought he must have imagined it.

"Let me up," she said, more firmly this time. The demand was still on the frail side, but he helped her to her feet anyway.

He made the mistake of leaving his hand on her arm too long, and she brushed it away roughly, staggering with the effort. He thought about just letting her fall, but reached out and caught her again. This time, she didn't resist. Of course, she didn't look at him either.

He took her hand and placed it up on the pommel of the saddle, telling her to hang on. He gave Pete's girth a firm snugging, and swung up top, then pulled the girl up behind him. Once he was sure she wasn't going to fall off and that she had a fair grip on his middle, he clucked to the horse.

As the appy walked on, and the girl's breasts rubbed into his back—he'd forgotten that, how could he forget a thing like that?—Slocum said, a little more gruffly than he intended, "Next time you're about to heat-stroke, tell somebody."

There was a pause before she said, "You're from the South."

The question—come to think of it, it was more a statement of fact—took him by surprise. What was it with this girl?

He said, "Alabama. But it's been a long time."

"Obviously. Long enough that you've lost your manners."

That did it. He reined in Pete and cranked around in the saddle so that he could see her face. "Well, if you aren't about the snottiest little—"

"Bitch?" she said, finishing the sentence for him. She smiled, but it was all mouth and no eyes. "That's right, Mr. Slocum. And it's something that would be a mistake on your part to forget."

The false smile slipped away, replaced by a look that was hard enough to cut glass. "I've hired you to find my Daddy Jim, and your payment does in no way include what I saw in your eyes back there. Now, start this horse moving."

If she was trying to intimidate him, it didn't work. She'd have to be quintuplets—and armed to the teeth—before he'd even start to feel edgy.

But there was fifteen hundred dollars at stake, so he said, "Oh, yes, ma'am. Pardon me all to hell, ma'am. And pardon me for *saying* 'hell,' ma'am. I'll start this old cayuse moving right this second."

And then he spurred the stud from a standing start into a flat-out run.

She yelped and almost lost her seat, but she clung to him tighter, squeezing those hard little breasts into his back while he grinned like an idiot, the hot wind whistling past his ears.

"Stop it!" he heard her cry, although the wind snatched away most of it. "Mr. Slocum! For the love of . . . Stop!"

He would have let the stud run for another minute or two, just to teach her a lesson, but something up ahead, something sprawled on their path, caused him to rein the horse to a skidding stop. The appy slid to a standstill in a cloud of choking dust, half-rearing, his hind-quarters tucked beneath him.

She started in again. "Of all the—"

"Shut up."

"How *dare* you tell me—"

"Be quiet."

"I will not! Who do you think you are to tell—"

"Shut up!" he repeated, with more command this time, and punctuated it with a hard slap to her upper thigh.

She shut up.

He nudged the horse forward twenty feet, then halted. "Get down," he said.

She slid off the horse without a word. He followed, pulling his Winchester from the scabbard, and signaled her to stay put.

She nodded mutely. She'd seen it too.

Slocum approached the body slowly. It would take more fingers and toes than he had to count the times a "dead" man had rolled over and fired—or tried to fire—up at him. He poked at the corpse with the barrel of his rifle. A rattly groan rose from it. Not quite a corpse yet.

Still holding the rifle on him, Slocum nudged the man over on his back with the toe of his boot. He was young, no more than twenty, and sandy-haired with a weedy mustache. His holster was empty, but somebody else's hadn't been, for a jagged hole pierced his blood-soaked flannel shirt.

He was barely breathing, but his eyelids fluttered.

Satisfied that this was no trick, Slocum called to the girl to bring up Pete, then knelt beside the dying boy. She positioned the stud so that his bulk threw some shade, and then, without being told, she handed the canteen down to Slocum. As he twisted the cap off, he decided that he was going to have to remember that slap-on-the-leg trick. Did wonders.

He held the canteen to the boy's mouth. At last the boy took a sip, but the attempt was feeble—more water ran down his chin than went into his gullet. Slocum knew he'd come too late. The boy was dying.

"Ambush," the boy whispered. "It . . . *ban-*

didos.'' Feebly, he sucked at the canteen, but coughed up the water, followed by quite a bit of blood that bubbled out over his chin, thick and dark. "They . . . they . . ."

And then the boy looked up, away from Slocum. He narrowed his eyes, as if struggling to make them focus, and then he breathed, "Aw, shit."

They were his final words.

Slocum turned his head toward the last thing the boy had seen before he died. And saw the sour countenance of Miss Maddie O'Hara, arms crossed, foot tapping.

5

"Well?" she said. "What are you waiting for? Give me his hat."

That idiot, Slocum, just stared at her. The truth was that she was feeling so sick to her stomach and her head was pounding so hard that she would have had to get better to die, but she'd be damned if she'd show weakness. Not now. Not to this man. Not under these circumstances.

She glared down at him. "The hat?"

Without a word, Slocum pulled the boy's hat off and threw it at her. She caught it against her chest. She didn't like the way Slocum was looking at her, and she was running out of the strength to hold a glare for very long, so she peered into the hat.

Best to avoid his gaze as much as possible. Best to avoid pushing him too hard too. She could still feel the sting where the brute had slapped her leg.

Studying the hat, she said, "He was one of them."

"One of who?"

"One of the men who robbed us and took

43

the wagon and Daddy Jim," she snapped. God, her head hurt! "Who else could I possibly mean? He recognized me."

Slocum grumbled something under his breath as he stood and brushed the dust from his knees, and she knew better than to say anything. Instead, she watched as he dug through his pack and pulled out a small folding shovel, which explained at least one of the dents in her backside. He snapped it into working order, and started to dig a hole.

"Good God! You're not going to take the time to bury him, are you?"

He paused, looked up at her and scowled, then went back to digging.

"But they're getting away! It's plain to me, even if it isn't to you, that the bandits were ambushed by more bandits. Or something." She wobbled, but he didn't notice. She took a deep breath and tried to ignore the pounding in her head. "Daddy Jim might be lying out on the desert this very minute. He could be wounded. He could be close to death. Every second counts!"

He just kept digging.

She pointed at the shovel, although he didn't notice, didn't even look up. "It'll take ten years for you to dig a grave with that ridiculous thing in this soil!" Her voice was growing shrill, and she stopped, biting her lips.

He stabbed the shovel into the ground and

scooped up another small load of grit and gravel. "Make yourself useful," he said, without a trace of sympathy or understanding. "Go pick up some rocks. Big ones. Don't go reachin' under any bushes without poking 'em with a stick first." He twisted, looking at her over his shoulder. "And put on that damn hat."

She curled the brim in her fingers angrily. No one had ever treated her like this! Ordering her around like a common laborer! And no one had ever been this rude to her either, at least not in the last eight years or so, not since she'd started working for Felicity.

Well, she supposed she'd started it. Mean came back at you, whether you meant it or not, no matter how dizzy or headachy you felt, even if you knew you were going to throw up or pass out any second. Mean came back.

It crossed her mind that she'd never so much as thanked him for saving her life.

Too late now.

She said, "I was just checking it. The hat, I mean."

"For what?" he said. His expression bordered on amused, but didn't quite reach it. "Bear traps? Alligators?"

"Head lice, if you must know." She jerked the blanket-shawl from her shoulders, nearly falling over with the effort, and jammed the hat on her head. "It would appear to be free of vermin."

"Honey, a few lice are the least of your worries," he said, in a tone that made her think she ought to be worrying less about her head and more about what he had in mind.

And to think she'd fantasized about him yesterday, when he found her on the hill! She'd imagined herself walking around his camp naked! Naked indeed, in this sun, in this heat, and in front of the likes of him! Little Maddie O'Hara, always in charge, always calling the shots. Well, he was in charge now, he was calling the shots, and he'd be in charge of any games he cared to play.

If she got into trouble—and Slocum smelled to her like nothing but—there'd be no Felicity to ring for, no big burly bouncer to come to her aid.

She shivered, despite the sweat soaking her bodice, running down her legs under the tattered skirts.

Slocum scared her.

She'd made the right decision about him. Best to just keep on being nasty and mean and generally hard to get along with.

A solid-gold bitch.

"What?" Slocum said, jerking her back to reality.

When she didn't answer, he continued. "If you're back from dreamland, go and get some rocks. And don't forget to whack at the bushes."

Her hands curled into fists. Infuriating, the

man was infuriating! "But what about Daddy Jim?"

He stabbed the shovel into the hard soil again. "The longer you stand there jawin' about it, the longer this is going to take. Now, move."

He told her to sit down after she'd made only two trips with the rocks. She looked parboiled and exhausted, and he reminded himself that she'd passed out from the heat not that long ago. That, and he'd been a little rough on her, what with knocking her off the horse and all. Maybe he'd gone too far. To tell the truth, he didn't know how she was still on her feet. Likely doing it just to be nasty.

So he told her to sit down next to Pete, in the little pool of shade. He made her drink some water, and then he finished up the burying himself.

After he scraped a shallow groove in the hard desert floor, he went over the body. No papers, no keepsakes, not even a watch, engraved or otherwise, to give the boy a name.

At last, he rolled the corpse into the grave, threw dirt over him, and piled the rocks on top, to keep the coyotes out. Or so he hoped. He'd had to haul quite a number of rocks himself, few of which were big enough to discourage a determined coyote. But considering the limited resources, it was the best he could do.

By the time he finished, it was coming very close to noon, and the shade created by the sleepy-eyed appaloosa's bulk had shrunk back to a purply pool, square beneath the horse. Mindless of the blistering heat, the girl had dozed off on the ground, her hat askew, her hands pressed together under her cheek, her body curled in an almost fetal position.

He stepped over her carefully, thinking he'd let her sleep as long as possible—when she was unconscious, she was quiet anyway—and shoved the collapsed spade down into his pack. Then he pulled down the water bag and gave Pete another drink.

While the horse slaked his thirst, Slocum studied the girl. *Miss Maddie O'Hara*, he thought, *what's your story?*

He couldn't figure her out. Sometimes he got the notion she was a whore—maybe a high-priced one. The way she looked at him sometimes, when she didn't know he could see her. Like she was appraising him, the way he'd appraise a horse. At those times she looked just a little too knowledgeable for some homegrown virgin.

He figured high-priced because she talked too highfalutin for a girl from the cribs.

Just wishful thinking, though. What would a high-priced whore be doing out here, wearing a gingham dress and chasing after her daddy?

Sometimes he had her figured for a ranch

girl with a cantankerous attitude—actually, wherever she was from, her attitude left a lot to be desired. Maybe she'd been sent back East once upon a time, and had never gotten over it. Maybe what he was seeing was the veneer of some Boston or New York finishing school.

A whore would have been a damn sight friendlier, and more welcome. A lot more welcome, especially in these circumstances.

In either case, he'd about come to the conclusion that this Daddy Jim, whoever he was, wasn't the girl's father. At least, he had a feeling she was lying. Maybe Daddy Jim was a benefactor, maybe some shirttail relative, maybe someone who kept her. But if he was someone who kept her, why would he be taking her to meet good old Frank, her fiancé, who'd gotten tossed off a horse and landed on his brains?

Still, she hadn't seemed too upset about it.

The horse had stopped drinking, and Slocum absently hitched the bag back to the saddle. More important was what lay ahead. *Bandidos*, the boy had said. He'd been one of the original holdup men. Again, Slocum wondered why the robbers hadn't killed the girl's daddy and left him behind, along with Maddie and the guards. Why take him along?

Unless they planned a ransom. But that didn't figure—they already had fifteen thousand in gold.

Slocum filled his cheeks with air, then blew

it out with a *whoosh*. He expected to find a pretty raw scene down the trail, and wondered if Maddie was up to it. He pulled down the second canteen—the first was empty now—and took a long drink while he considered that scenario. Dead highwaymen and dead Daddy Jim, and the gold long gone, packed deep into Los Cuervos on the backs of Mexican ponies.

His fifteen hundred was looking like harder money all the time.

His gaze shifted down, to the girl. She was a genuine looker, all right; all the prettier when she was asleep and therefore not tossing orders or insults at him. For the first time he noticed that her mouth was bow-shaped, the sort of mouth that should have held a natural smile. At least it did while she was sleeping.

It struck him that she looked innocent, like a little girl, like an angel, until his gaze drifted down to her breasts, which strained the fabric of her bodice.

Not such a little girl. Not such an angel either. Jesus. Why did she have to be so blasted cantankerous all the time?

He nudged her with his boot. "Maddie?"

She smiled in her sleep, stirred slightly, and waved a hand limply at her face, as if brushing away a fly.

"Miss O'Hara?" he said louder.

She opened her eyes. She looked up at him. The smile turned into a grimace. She said, "Oh," as if she would rather have seen any face in the world but his. She sat up. "Are you done?"

An hour and a half of easy jog later, Slocum was standing in his stirrups, casting out over the territory ahead with his scope, when he sighted the scene of the raid beneath circling vultures.

He could see bodies—snatches of unnatural color in the brush anyway. There was a wagon too, turned on its side. One saddle horse grazed to the side, but that was all. The thieves hadn't stuck around long enough to catch it.

He sat back down in the saddle, then collapsed the scope and tucked it away.

"Well?" came the voice from behind him. "Did you spot anything?"

He pursed his lips, not knowing how to break it to her.

She pounded his back with a hard little fist. "Mr. Slocum! What was it?"

All right. She wanted it, she'd get it, and with no sugar-coating. He said, "An empty wagon and a bunch of bodies."

Behind him he felt her stiffen, and then there was a softer pressure on his back. Her forehead, he realized, to his surprise.

She said, quite softly, "Was there a big man? Not too tall, but big around?"

He gathered his reins and clucked to the stud, who moved out at a jog. "Too far.

Couldn't tell. We'll be there in ten minutes or so."

She tightened her grip on his waist, and grabbed fistfuls of his shirt. "No," she said, and Slocum would have sworn her voice was choked with tears. "Not in ten minutes."

This time it was she who sank her heels into the appy, kicking him into a dead run.

6

Several times she nearly lost her grip and landed in the scrub, but she didn't care. Neither, it seemed, did Slocum. Whether he was in a hurry to get to the wagon and the gold, or simply content to let her kill herself, didn't matter a whit. All that mattered was that he'd given the appaloosa its head. Urged on by her drumming heels, it ran. She slipped left, slipped right, the packs and saddlebags beneath her bruising her already sore behind.

Once, when the appy leapt over fallen saguaro, she lost her seat completely, her legs flying out behind her momentarily. Her grip on Slocum's middle was the only thing that saved her; had she slipped, she would have gone off over the horse's rump and into a pair of flying heels.

By the time they reached the wagon, the appy was lathered and blowing, and she slid down off him without being told. She hit the ground running, headed for the nearest body.

She knew, when she was still twenty-five feet away, that it wasn't Daddy Jim.

She went from body to body, mindless of

53

the buzzing flies. Carrion birds, ungainly on the ground, flopped away in angry, arguing clouds, just out of range, waiting for her to move so that they could resume feeding.

But despite the savaged faces of the corpses, she recognized none of them as Daddy Jim.

She sank to her knees in the scrub, tears of relief flooding her eyes. Alive! He was still alive. Sweet Daddy Jim, with his big belly and his harebrained schemes and his booming laugh; Daddy Jim, with that beautiful head, round and bald and shiny as a waxed billiard ball, and all those lovely double chins; the only man who had ever loved her just for herself, and not what she could do to him, not what she could make him feel.

Daddy Jim was alive, and nothing else mattered but that. There was a God after all.

She began to cry, and then she began to laugh, the sound of it scattering the vultures again. How long she sat there, laughing and crying and rocking back and forth on her knees, she didn't know. But suddenly a shadow fell over her.

Slocum.

She stopped laughing.

He was atop the stud, and he'd roped the stray saddle horse, a chestnut mare. The appaloosa whickered at her, and the mare, standing about ten feet back on the end of a taut rope, pinned her ears in a threat and twisted her neck, biting the air.

Slocum was high above her. He looked down, his saddle leather creaking. The sun was behind him and she couldn't read his face, but his voice, when it came, was hateful. As usual.

He said, "Since you think this is so all-fired hilarious, you can help me dig the graves."

Slocum put the last rock on the final grave. The sun was low on the horizon, and he stood looking at it for a moment, giving another swipe to his face and neck with his bandanna.

Maddie had run out of steam early on, and was slumped, peevishly, beside the wagon. It had been thrown on its side, making a good sunbreak (and potential firewood) but little else. One of the axles was broken, a side was smashed, and a wheel hung in two pieces, the spokes jutting at sick angles.

The bandits had taken all the horses except the chestnut mare and one of the team, a wheel horse. It was dead. He supposed he should burn it—he'd already dug more than his share of graves for one day, and he had no intention of burying a damn horse. Not without a winch anyway. But he couldn't burn it, not without setting fire to half the territory.

He expected the vultures would have a feast tomorrow to make up for the one they'd lost today.

The bandits had been in a hurry. They'd left behind three of the wagon's water bags, a ten-pound bag of oats, and some food. Probably ran out of room, what with all that gold to carry, he thought sullenly. They probably had a hideout close by, if they'd left the water.

His gaze shifted to Los Cuervos. That was where their tracks were headed for. Great, just great. Hills, then steep bluffs and death-trap canyons. A favorite stronghold of the Apaches, and now a place of safety for Mexican *bandidos* who crossed over the border to raid.

He'd buried four white men and a Mexican at this place. The Mexican had been dressed in the manner of a *bandido*. He suspected that the four whites, along with the boy he'd covered over earlier, had been the original gang of thieves.

He knew how they'd done it; at least he thought he had a pretty good idea. The *bandidos* must have waited for the wagon on the other side of the small knoll they'd passed. When the wagon came alongside the knoll, they'd opened fire. Probably dropped the boy there and never checked to make sure he was dead. Half a mile later, the wagon had hit a rock and landed on its side. The *bandidos* had finished off the survivors at their leisure, and suffered only one casualty.

Except that the girl's daddy wasn't there.

This whole thing gave him a bad feeling. *Bandidos* didn't much care for gringos. In fact, most of them treated whites the way Apaches treated Mexicans: with no mercy whatsoever. Why would a band of cutthroats take Daddy Jim along? Stake him out on a red anthill with his eyelids slashed, yes. Rope him to a wagon wheel and burn him alive, certainly. It was all for sport.

Of course, they hadn't taken the time to play with the first batch of thieves. The worst one he'd seen had taken two bullets, to the leg and shoulder, and there was a third and final shot through his head. But still, this was twice the old man had been held up, and twice he'd been spared and taken along.

It just didn't make sense.

Right now, all he knew for certain was that he was tired and hungry. He turned toward the wagon, toward the girl.

Jesus, you'd think she would have made camp! You'd think she'd have a fire going, and supper cooking, and hot coffee ready. A man would think she would've made herself useful.

But no, she was still sitting in the same spot, in the same position, her hands folded in her lap. Something about the way she was sitting there—or maybe it was something about having dug six graves in one day—got his back up, and before he knew it he was beside the wagon, and pulling her up by one arm.

She snarled, "Can we go now?"

Which was exactly the wrong thing to say to Slocum at that moment.

His eyes narrowed. "Of all the—"

"Unhand me!" she screeched, and took a swing at him. And missed. "Don't you dare touch me, you . . . you . . . you grave digger!"

He had half a mind to give her arm a good twist, but instead, he threw her to the ground in exasperation. "You don't know what's good for you, lady. I could have been digging a hole for *you* yesterday. And I would have too. I've got too much respect for the coyotes to poison them."

"Ha!" She climbed to her feet. "You're stalling, that's what you're doing!"

"I'm not—"

"You don't want to catch up with them at all! You're afraid!"

"If you had any sense—"

"You're a coward! A coward!"

That did it. "And you, lady, are a ringtailed hog-scalder of a bitch."

"Bastard!" She threw herself at him, fists pounding his chest. "Sonofabitching bastard!"

He pushed her away, but she came right back and slapped his face, hard. "You pig! I'd be better off on my own than with the likes of you!"

Slocum did the only thing he could think of, in the circumstances. He grabbed her arm, dropped down to one knee, pulled her over the other one, and smacked her fanny with his open hand. There was a gratifying *pop* even through her skirts, and it made him feel so good that he did it again.

She was still screeching, calling him names—calling his whole family names—using words that one very seldom heard from a lady, and fighting like a bobcat in a gunnysack. He pinned her down with his left elbow and gave her two more good whacks across her backside.

She stopped struggling. She lay there for a second, panting and limp. And then she suddenly twisted to the side with all her strength.

It wasn't enough, though. Slocum caught her and pulled her back and swatted her again, this time pinning her arm against her back.

Now they were both panting. Through clenched teeth, Slocum said, "Damn it, you're not getting up until you behave."

She made a little grunting wiggle, which was all she could manage against Slocum's grip.

Slocum's jaw muscles worked. Low, he growled, "Say it."

There was a pause. He could hear her labored breath. Was she crying too, and for real this time? And then finally, she said very softly, "All right, damn you. I'll behave."

He relaxed his grip, letting her slide to the ground, and then he stood up, feeling just a little ashamed of himself.

She was on all fours now, head lowered and

sobbing, and suddenly Slocum was worried. Had he really hurt her? Not that she didn't deserve it, but still . . .

"Look," he said, putting a hand down to her, "I'm sorry. I don't go around hitting women. It's just that you made me so—"

She came straight up with her fist cocked, and slugged him square in the jaw. The force of it—and the surprise—staggered him back a step.

"I lied, you stupid bastard!" she said, her voice shrill. "You want someone to 'behave,' go rent yourself a Mexican whore. Did you know you mumble in your sleep?" She tipped her head to one side and rolled her eyes, mimicking him. " 'Oh, Consuelo. Oh, honey, yes, that's good.' "

Slocum felt heat rising up his neck. He also felt unaccountably angry. He started, "Why, you—"

"She can cook for you and take your orders and your abuse too," she snapped, cutting him off. "But you work for me, remember? You're nothing but a hired hand, and I won't be spanked like some child or knocked off horses or sassed back or made to walk anymore. And I swear to God, if you hit me again I'll get a gun and blow your balls into next week."

He grabbed for her angrily, not sure what he was going to do, but she ducked, making a quick pivot, and then she was on him again, slapping him, pounding her fists against his shoulders and cursing him.

He caught her left wrist, tried to catch her right wrist, and missed.

"You big, dumb sonofabitch," she screeched, and went to slap him again, but this time he grabbed her wrist before she could land the blow.

They stood there in the fading light, Slocum imprisoning her arms. Her body, her heaving breasts, were tight against him, her nostrils flared with exertion. Her head was tilted back, her throat exposed. Their eyes locked, hers tear-filled and angry, but quickly—and strangely—changing in expression. They grew half-lidded, almost drowsy, yet still full of fire.

He growled, "You little wildcat."

Her lips parted. She whispered, "Fuck me, Slocum."

7

Slocum was so startled at the order that he forgot, for a moment, to be shocked. Still gripping her wrists, he pushed her out at arm's length. "What?"

Her lips quivering, her bosom rising and falling rapidly, she whispered, "You heard me. Take me now. Right here."

He was suddenly aware of the erection straining his britches. When the hell had that happened? But he summoned all his self-control. She was crazy! Did she expect him to provide sex on command, like some damned trained donkey in a border show? Given half a chance, she'd shoot him in his sleep and tear off after her Daddy Jim and get herself raped or killed or both. Which would be no skin off his nose, except that he'd be dead too.

He said, "Look, lady, I don't usually go around . . . hell, I'm no woman-beater. If that's the kind of thing that hitches your horse, I don't want to play, you got that?"

Her gaze traveled down to his crotch, then came back up to meet his eyes. She licked her lips, just the tip of her tongue darting out, but her expression remained unchanged.

Crazy. Peach-orchard crazy, and he was stuck with her.

She purred, "You sure?"

He said, "I am. Now, I'm going to let go of you. Don't go hitting me again." He started to ease his grip on her wrists, then added, "I won't knock you off the horse again. And I won't hit you if you don't hit me first, but you've got to help around here, all right? And don't say . . . don't say that word. It's not lady-like."

He couldn't believe what he was saying, couldn't believe what he was doing. He couldn't believe that he was bothered by a word like that coming from her lips. Maybe it was because they were such pretty lips. All he knew was that his erection was fading, and he was tired and hungry and out of sorts, and wanted nothing so much as a meal, and to sit down while he ate it.

Maybe if she'd made the offer when he was feeling a little less like he'd been ridden hard and put up wet . . .

He let go of her, and she took a step back. Straightened. Stiffened. Her eyes were clear again, piercing.

She said, "I offer my gravest apologies, Mr. Slocum. I don't know what came over me. I hope you'll forget all about this matter. And now, if you'll excuse me, I'll see about dinner." Then she actually curtsied—curtsied!—

and turned and walked away toward the piled packs and saddlebags.

Slocum stared after her, rubbing the new sore spot on his jaw, half-wondering if he'd imagined what had just happened. From bitch to hellcat to come-hither whore to schoolmarm, all in the course of half an hour. It boggled the mind.

He stood there a moment longer in the fading light, and then he muttered, "Oh, the hell with it." He headed back over to the wagon, to start collecting broken boards for the fire.

He'd never figure her out. And right now, he was too exhausted to try.

Maddie sat beside the wagon. She scrubbed the last of the tin plates with sand, wiped it clean, and stuck it in the pack with the others, all the time eyeing Slocum.

Dinner had been a silent affair, full of sideways looks, and after dinner, he'd shaved while she cleaned up the supper mess. She saw the folded blade and the little mirror on the rock beside him, the soap and brush beside them, drying. He poked at the fire with a stick, then held up the glowing end to light another cigarette. What did he call them? Quirlies, that was it. Queer sort of name.

He was an odd duck, this Slocum, with his quirlies instead of cigarettes, and his lucifers instead of sulphur tips, his hard face and his soft Alabama drawl. And this bizarre penchant he had to stop and bury people he didn't even know.

But chastity? She couldn't believe she'd offered, couldn't believe the fight had aroused her as much as it had.

Most of all, she couldn't believe he'd turned her down.

She'd slipped out of her role, and in a big way, but she couldn't control herself, couldn't stop the words. And afterwards, she'd slipped into another role. Now she was stuck with it.

She'd never claimed to be much of an actress, but for fifty dollars, you did whatever the client wanted. It had been easy—and at first, it had seemed most expedient—for her to slip into the role of the wicked bitch. Back when she was with Felicity, Father Reynolds had come to see her every two weeks, and that was what he'd wanted. Someone to boss him around and be nasty to him and insult him and call him names, and make him clean the floor with his tongue and fingers. He'd never touched her, bless his sick old heart, but he'd left the floor sparkling.

It hadn't worked on Slocum, though.

Well, it had, in a way. He'd been keeping his distance. But he'd also been making her walk, and dumping her off that blasted horse and slapping back. Hard. Maybe she'd been right to change tactics. Not the way she'd done it, of course. No, not that way. Despite the cool night air, she felt heat seep into her cheeks, remembering what she'd said, the way she'd said it.

God.

Why did he have to be so big and strong and capable? Why did he have to be so... *male*? After all, she reminded herself, making excuses again, it had been two years since she'd been with a man, and two years was an awfully long time.

No. Best not to think about him. Best to keep her thoughts on tomorrow, on Daddy Jim. She played a part with him too—the dutiful daughter, Daddy's precious pearl. He'd liked the act, so she'd just kept it up, fearful that he wouldn't like her the way she really was. After all, wasn't Daddy Jim sweet and kind? Hadn't he saved her life?

"Not a sign of consumption," the young Arizona doctor had concluded, not eight months after Daddy'd brought her south.

"You see, sweet pea?" Daddy Jim had said, smiling next to her in the jouncing buckboard seat, patting her knee kindly. "You catch it early enough, and it's gone forever! As long as you stay in Arizona, that is."

Frankly, she'd never heard of consumption being cured so quickly—if at all, come to think of it—but if there had been a miracle, she was glad it had happened to her.

And so she'd stayed on, mending his socks and learning to cook his fancy meals—she'd become quite the gourmet cook on Daddy

Jim's account—and helping around the place. She'd learned to poach fruit and mend tack and filet a snake and patch up the help when they needed patching.

She'd learned to call herself O'Hara, his last name—so people wouldn't talk, he'd said, although they never saw any people at all. He'd had to drive all day to take her to town to see the doctor that time.

But she hadn't minded. She hadn't been all that attached to Maddie Sewell. She hadn't minded the isolation either. It was nice, after the hustle and bustle of a busy Chicago gaming house. Well, she kept telling herself it was nice. There were the panners and sluicers to talk to, but most of all, there was Daddy Jim.

He needed her, depended on her. He was old. He was fat and ungainly too, and couldn't get around much anymore. He sat on the porch most of the day, scribbling things in a notebook that he snapped shut whenever she came near. She didn't mind that either, though. He needed someone to look after him, poor sweet thing, living as he did on that godforsaken ranch out in the middle of nowhere and not a cow or calf in sight.

There was a bit of a mystery to Daddy Jim, but she hadn't asked questions. She'd found a place where she fit in at last, even if she'd played so many roles in her life that she wasn't sure who she was anymore, and there she intended to stay. Maybe with Daddy Jim she could figure it out.

Except that once again, she'd gotten herself stuck in a role.

Except that now he'd disappeared, and by rights, should have been dead twice.

Puzzling.

But then, Daddy Jim could talk the wrens out of the cactus. Poetry came spilling forth from those pink lips. Like a baby's mouth, she'd always thought, a cherub's. Poetry and flimflam flowed from him. He could bamboozle God.

She snuck another glance at Slocum, and found him looking toward her. Why did he have to be so tall, so handsome? And . . . decent!

She came to the belated conclusion that he could have raped her—*really* raped her, nothing like the fantasy at all—and then slashed her throat at any time. And when she'd acted like an ass—a crazy, sex-starved idiot was more like it—he'd pushed her away. And apologized for hitting her!

She wanted him. She wanted him so badly that she could feel the dampness between her legs again, and that old, familiar burning, low in her belly. And she knew he'd wanted her. She'd seen the way those pants were stretched tight through the crotch. Stretched awfully tight, come to think about it. She swallowed, then bit at her lip.

It had been such a long time.

Don't think about it.

She stood up. "Mr. Slocum?" she called primly. "Did you say we had a surplus of water?"

He paused. "A little."

Golden light from the fire washed up over his face. She could see him clearly, and was grateful that he couldn't see her nearly so well, for she found that she was flushed again.

"Might I have enough to wash in?" Lord, why couldn't she leave this prissy spinster role behind? Why couldn't she find out who she was, really and honestly, and be that, all the time? Just plain Maddie O'Hara. Maddie Sewell.

He looked at her oddly, then shrugged. "Be my guest."

"Thank you," she said, and with a groan, picked up a bag of water.

It was only three quarters full, but a good bit heavier than she'd expected. She struggled around to the backside of the fallen wagon, half dragging it. You'd never guess how much they weighed, she thought, by the casual way he tossed them around.

Strong. Strong and good-looking and tall and broad-shouldered, and with those green eyes . . .

Don't think about it.

• • •

Slocum poked the fire and tried not to look at her. The idiot had said "wash," but she was taking a full-fledged, stark-naked bath. Not that he could see her. Not that he had to.

She'd neatly laid out her clothes along the upturned side of the wagon, and she was humming softly, an old tune called "Was My Brother in the Battle." Her head and pale, naked shoulders disappeared, then reappeared, then disappeared again as she bathed, and he could imagine the firm, high breasts, the silky stomach, the water coursing down her body into secret crevices. . . .

He reached for the coffeepot, and dropped it just as suddenly, shaking the heat out of his hand. Under his breath, he growled, "Sonofabitch," then righted the coffeepot, this time wrapping his bandanna around his hand.

Order him around, would she?

He didn't need this. He didn't need her money. He doubted there'd be any money to find, after this last robbery. He didn't need her, his erection to the contrary.

He willed his cock down. Again. Which didn't take much effort. His ass was dragging, all right.

Angrily, he dug in his pocket for his fixings. He'd be out of tobacco if he didn't ration it, but he had to do something, had to get his mind off Maddie O'Hara.

She changed tunes. Now she was humming "Hard Times Come Again No More," and it made him mad, for no discernible reason.

He shoved the tobacco pouch and papers back into his pocket, and was about to yell at her to hurry up, dammit, and be quiet about it, when a cry, thin and distant, rang through the night.

"Hullo the camp!"

Slocum rolled out of the firelight, then got to his feet and moved further away, his Winchester cocked and ready. He didn't need this now. A glance at the wagon showed him that Maddie had ducked down and out of sight. Finally, she'd done something sensible.

The rider was dimly silhouetted in the distance on a low-headed horse. "Hullo the camp!" he called again. "Sure could use some coffee for me and water for my horse!"

Satisfied that the man was alone, Slocum answered, "Ride on in and help yourself," but he kept the Winchester on target.

The newcomer slowly rode up into the firelight and reined in. He rode a badly used buckskin, and under the dust, he was dressed like a German banker, albeit a skinny one, in a black suit and a plain vest. A gold watch chain, studded with fobs, winked beneath the open sides of the coat.

He looked at the rifle, then looked at Slocum. He smiled, gesturing at the upturned wagon. "Have some trouble?"

Slocum didn't return the smile. "Another pack of folks. They got hit by *bandidos.*"

"Mind if I get down?"

Slocum had a sour feeling about this fellow. "Suit yourself. What brings you out here?"

Leaving his horse to stand, the man went to the fire and scooped up Slocum's empty cup. Before Slocum could warn him, he picked up the pot barehanded and poured out a cup. He set it down casually, then sucked his fingers where they'd touched the hot metal.

He said, still smiling, "I might ask you the same thing. Sort of the middle of nowhere, isn't it?"

They both turned at the sound of a twig's snap. There, at the edge of the fire's circle of light, stood Miss Maddie O'Hara. She was in her underwear, and she looked madder than a shaved bear.

Slocum figured she'd finally gone all the way crazy, and moved to the side, saying softly, "Now, Maddie . . ."

She stared at the new arrival, eyes narrowed, hands balled into fists. She said, "Frank? You're supposed to be dead!"

Good old Frank? The deceased fiancé? This was getting interesting. Slocum relaxed a little. Maybe she'd pound on Frank for a while, although Slocum doubted Frank would feel it if that coffeepot was any indication.

Frank said, "You're supposed to be in Halcyon!"

"Well, I'm not, am I? I'm out here trying to

find Daddy Jim. Because you weren't there to help him, he's been kidnapped."

Frank held his ground. "Why didn't you wait in Halcyon?"

In the shadows and ignored, Slocum raised a brow. Frank wasn't surprised by the kidnapping. He was madder that Maddie wasn't in Halcyon, although it was obvious he hadn't gone there searching for her.

The girl pressed her lips together. "Why didn't you look for me there? They said you were dead. They said a horse threw you."

That was another thing. Maddie didn't seem even slightly glad to see him resurrected.

"An exaggeration," Frank said, and offered no further explanation. His voice had a quality that got Slocum's back up, like grit and oil, and the man's eyes were flickery, funny. He'd hold them still for a second, and then they'd dance all around before they lit again.

"You weren't supposed to go on to Caballo Loco with Jim," Frank said, his voice rising. More grit, less oil. The eyes flashed left and right, wiggled a jig, then steadied on Maddie. "You were supposed to wait in Halcyon, Maddie, not go gallivanting around on the desert with some saddle tramp! And in your goddamn underwear!"

Maddie pulled herself up and audibly drew a breath. "Don't you *dare* use foul language in my presence, Frank Osborn!"

Slocum, still outside the light, slowly shook

his head. She cussed like a two-bit whore in front of him, but got mad at a measly little "goddamn" from Frank? It was like watching a bad play.

The rifle swinging at his side, he stepped forward. "Mind if the saddle tramp says something?"

They both wheeled toward him and barked, "What!"

"You," he said, wearily pointing his rifle in the general direction of Frank, "go see to your horse, because he's about to keel over. There're oats and water yonder. And then you bunk over there." He indicated a place next to the wagon.

"And you." He pointed toward Maddie. "You go put on the rest of your clothes and go to sleep. Here or with Frank or in New Mexico, I don't care. I'm too damn tired to mess with either one of you tonight."

8

Slocum woke groggily just before the break of first light, and winced at his sore shoulder. He was puzzled for the half second it took him to remember digging the graves.

The fire had gone out. He sat up slowly in blue-gray shadows, easing the knots and kinks out of his body, then stood up, carefully stretching. He'd been hard on his body these past years, and the various parts woke up independently, in their own time.

By the time he finished relieving himself, he was most of the way awake. He headed toward the wagon to pry off some more planks for firewood, and to kick Frank and Maddie awake. She must have cozied up to him during the night.

Talk in his sleep indeed!

He was halfway there when he realized they were gone. And worse, his horse and supplies were gone with them! They'd taken the ammunition, the water, the food, everything, and left behind only what they couldn't steal or carry—one water bag, the things he'd kept by his side as he slept, and Frank's lousy excuse for a horse.

The buckskin gelding eyed him warily.

At least they hadn't made off with his guns. He'd kept his Colts and the Winchester with him as he slept, as always. Those, and his saddlebags. Among the contents was one box, half empty, of cartridges, a few scraps of jerky, and a bite or two of hardtack.

Normally, he would have just said the hell with those two, they deserved each other. He would have left them to the *bandidos*, and gone back up the trail to Yuma. After all, there was more water a day away, and he could live off the land. But they'd stolen his horse.

And nobody stole his horse.

Nobody.

He watered the sorry buckskin and staked him out on a long tether line, so he could at least graze on what meager fodder the desert offered. Then he went back to the campsite and, with short, sharp motions, began to roll up his blankets.

She wasn't so sure this was a good idea.

First of all, Frank's story didn't make sense. Oh, he'd been really sweet, later on last night, explaining it. He said it must have been a mix-up in the names, and another man must have died up north. But how many Frank Weatherwax Osborns could there be in Arizona, and why in the world would anyone think to tell her about the other one?

He'd seemed angry to find her with Slocum. She supposed he was mad to find her on the desert, and with another man, not to mention in her underwear. That, she supposed, she could understand.

But if Frank thought that she thought he was alive and well, and that she was waiting for him in Halcyon, why hadn't he gone looking for her there? What was *he* doing on the desert?

After all, they were supposed to be married upon Daddy Jim's return from the smelter.

It came to her, belatedly, that she'd explained herself to him, but not the other way around. She'd told him that Daddy Jim *had* left her in town. He'd gotten her a hotel room and left her there, supposedly to mourn Frank. He'd said the trip was too fatiguing, too dangerous for his little dewdrop. She'd waited a half day, then paid a cowhand twenty dollars to gallop her after the wagon. Daddy Jim had given in, although he hadn't looked one bit happy about it.

But Frank had never explained why he hadn't even passed through Halcyon.

She looked at him now, riding slightly ahead on Slocum's big appaloosa. It was obvious the horse was too much for him. The stud had been fractious and uncharacteristically skittish all day, alternately prancing and snaking his head and giving little crow hops.

Frank's solution for everything was to smack him over the head with a stick.

Her mare wasn't much better behaved. She bared her teeth at the stud every time he came within range, and she'd tried to reach up and nip Frank's leg more times than Maddie could count.

She was beginning to think the horse was smarter than she was.

They'd entered the low hills about an hour ago. Long stretches of burning sun were relieved by longer periods of deep gray-purple shadow as they traveled down through the valleys, down into what was rapidly becoming a canyon, maybe a series of canyons. It was hard to tell. All she knew was that she was already lost.

Frank stopped the appaloosa. He mopped his brow, then took a drink from his canteen.

"Get that mare away," he snapped, when she brought her horse up beside him. "She's coming in season. Driving him crazy."

Maddie moved the mare a safe distance away from the stud, then slipped from the saddle. The ground felt good under her feet. At least it wasn't moving.

"What are you doing?" Frank eyed her suspiciously. That was another thing. She'd awakened to find Frank saddling the stud. He'd said he was going to wake her, ask her to come along. But was he? He'd been crotchety all morning.

"Watering the horses," she said, struggling to get the water bag down without dropping it. It seemed that Slocum knew what he was doing, and yesterday he'd watered his horse about mid-morning. She got the bag open and, resting the butt end on the ground, held the top wide enough so that the mare could dip her nose down into it.

Frank made no move to get down, so after the mare finished drinking, Maddie dragged the bag over to the appy and offered it to him.

"You're crazy," Frank said, wiping at his neck.

"I think Daddy Jim is the crazy one." She looked up. "Why he'd be so set on my getting married to you is beyond me."

Frank jerked the appy's head up, away from the water, spilling part of it. "Because—"

The appy reared slightly, nearly dumping Frank to the brush, and she thought that Slocum wouldn't have been so sloppy, Slocum was a horseman. She wished again that she hadn't listened to Frank. He'd get her killed long before they found Daddy Jim. Slocum might be a rude bastard, but at least he knew what he was doing. And his eyes didn't dart willy-nilly around the countryside, like Frank's did. Had they done that before?

"Never mind," Frank said, having gotten

the horse reasonably under control. For the time being. "We're almost there."

She'd thought they were just following the tracks, that they'd come on Daddy Jim and the bandits and then . . . Well, she wasn't sure what would happen then. "We're almost where?"

Frank gave a sigh of exasperation. "To your precious Daddy."

"But—"

"Just shut up and get on the horse and ride."

Her eyes narrowed. "What did you say?"

Frank seemed to think better of it. His expression softened, then warmed. "Sorry, my dear. The heat's getting to me, I guess. Up on the horse now, there's a good girl."

She mounted on the second try, after she got the mare to stand still, and stared at him. Confusing, very confusing. What did he mean he was taking her to Daddy Jim? Why wasn't he afraid in these canyons?

Slocum wouldn't have been afraid, but at least he would have been wary.

Slocum would have been watching for any little thing that was out of order.

Slocum would have taken care of her.

Frank gathered his reins. "There, precious. That's better. It's nice to have a palouse horse again." He patted the stud's neck gingerly, as if he were afraid of it. "Shall we?" He squeezed the stud with his heels—too hard, for the horse bolted and, with one hand clamped to the saddlehorn, Frank reined in clumsily. Finally the appy was under control again, and they started ahead.

"Are you sure he won't follow?" she asked, hoping that he would.

"Who?"

"Slocum!"

Frank laughed. "On that piece of buzzard bait I left him? He's got no supplies, hardly any water, and that old plug of a buckskin. No, I promise you he cut over to Oro Tiempo, probably on foot."

"Oh," she said, but she kept her eyes on that appaloosa's backside.

Frank didn't know Slocum. Slocum didn't strike her as a man who loved many things, but Slocum loved that horse. He took better care of it than he did of himself. It ate before he ate, drank before he drank, rested while he toiled.

She'd never loved anybody or anything like that, except for her mama, God rest her soul, and Daddy Jim. She'd barely known Frank when Daddy Jim announced her engagement. She'd said yes because she loved the old man, and it was a marriage. She didn't want Daddy Jim to die and suddenly find herself an old, broken-down whore with nowhere to go. Frank had seemed aloof when she'd met him, the one time he'd come to the ranch, but she'd thought he was shy.

That wasn't it at all, she was coming to realize. He had as many roles, as many games and characters, as she did. She didn't know what sort, exactly, but she had the feeling that his were dangerous.

So she kept her mouth shut and kept her eyes ahead, on the appaloosa, and sank back into the role of dutiful fiancée, adoring daughter. John Slocum wouldn't come for her—she'd made sure of that with her bitching and moaning and ordering him about. How could she have been so stupid!

No, Slocum wouldn't come for her. She had a feeling, though, that he'd come for his horse, even if he had to crawl to do it.

The buckskin was nearly used up.

Slocum walked beside him, following the trail, wishing he'd walk up on a patch of wild oats.

Fat chance.

He was well into the hills now, and moving carefully. Frank and Maddie hadn't tried to cover their tracks. They were plain, imposed over the imprints of the *bandidos*, and the two weren't moving fast, which was good for him and the bony buckskin.

Since morning, he'd ridden an hour, walked an hour, ridden an hour, and now it was early afternoon. He found a place they'd stopped. A scuffle of the stud's hooves in the dust. Maddie's footprints, but not Frank's.

He bent down and ran a gloved hand over the dirt. Gritty clay clumped together where a horse had relieved itself. No, where someone had spilled water. She'd watered the horses?

No. She'd probably stopped to take a goddamn bath.

A wave of anger passed through him as he thought about it, about her, but he quickly tamped it down. He had to keep a cool head, especially now, when the land was beginning to twist and dip into canyons.

He moved on.

Their tracks headed down now, into the depths of the canyon maze. Slocum kept to the shadows, which were growing deeper as the afternoon wore on, leading the buckskin, following the trail.

He came to a narrow passage and stopped, eyeing it leerily. He was deep inside the canyon system now. In fact, he couldn't see the hills behind him any longer at all, just crumbling canyon walls behind. Before him was a narrow passage, water- and wind-cut through solid stone.

He'd been walking the buckskin long enough. He checked the canyon rims one more time, then mounted and started into the passage, his rifle before him.

The walls were swirled limestone, reddish orange and brown and cream, turned dark and bluish by the shadows which engulfed the passage. The smooth walls undulated, coming in close, sinking back a few feet, then narrowing so tightly that his knees threatened to scrape both sides. He wondered how the hell Frank had made it through on the appy.

Echoes. Each footfall of shod hoof on stone sounded like two hundred in the narrow, twisting corridor. If the *bandidos* were waiting up ahead, he might just as well send a brass band to announce himself. He reined in the buckskin. He should have led the horse in, but it was too late. Before the echoes dimmed, Slocum started backing the buckskin up.

After fifteen very slow feet of skinning his rump and shoulders on the stone sides he couldn't see, the horse refused to back up anymore, and no amount of coercion would convince him otherwise. Slocum couldn't say he blamed him. Well, either he could stay stuck in this passage for the rest of his life, or he could move forward. He started ahead again, cautiously.

After several minutes of twisting and turning, he saw light up ahead. He brought the buckskin to within five feet of the point where the passage suddenly opened out into the light, into a much broader canyon, and sat in the shadows as the echoes behind him faded.

It looked quiet. Through the narrow opening, he saw a hawk reel in the bright sky. Farther out, on the canyon floor, a jackrabbit winked into view, then was gone. Slowly, his

Winchester raised, he started forward, into the light.

Hands grabbed him, pummeled him, pulled him from his horse, wrenched his rifle away, knocked him to the ground, and pinned his arms and legs, all in a heartbeat, before he could fight back.

As he blinked up into the sunlight, the *bandidos*, five or six of them, crowded around him. "*Como esta, gringo?*" said a guttural voice.

And then a rifle butt crashed into his skull, and everything went black.

9

He roused to a slow, sore burn in his belly and a fiery ache in his head. The view was all wrong, and it took him a second to realize they hadn't killed him—yet.

They'd tied him over his horse, and they were proceeding, single file so far as he could tell, along a steep path that hugged the side of a cliff. Very steep, and very precarious. His head hung out over the edge of the trail, and all he could see was a thirty-foot drop. He held very still, and prayed the buckskin wouldn't stumble.

The chain of horses followed the path downward, twisting through a hairpin curve that turned into an S. Slocum's captors were for the most part silent, although he could hear occasional mumbles in Spanish coming from back in the line, mostly men talking to their mounts, reassuring them.

And then, after a sudden, terrifying skid down a gravelly slope, they were down on the flat. The last of the riders swarmed around him in a pack, breaking their horses into a gallop and shouting. The frightened buckskin was pulled along with the rest, through a long, rock-walled, shadowed passage, then out into the light again. The saddle punched into Slocum's middle again, and all he could see was the dust that stung his eyes and clogged his nose.

They stopped as quickly as they'd started. Men jumped down from the saddles, and he could hear voices, many voices speaking rapid-fire Spanish, though all he could see was dust and legs, and then someone was sawing at his ropes. Abruptly, he felt someone yank him down from the buckskin. He landed on the ground sputtering and on his side, his hands and feet still bound.

The *bandidos* who'd brought him in ignored him now. They led their horses away, joking amongst themselves, and as the dust settled, Slocum found himself sprawled in the dirt, rather uncomfortably, before an adobe hacienda.

He was surprised to find the building here, even more surprised that it was not the only one. There were several other structures that resembled nothing so much as mud-brick barracks, long and narrow and windowed on only one side, and numerous wattle-sided ramadas with open fronts. Many horses milled in the corrals, and Slocum caught a glimpse of copper spots. Old Pete, he knew, with a sigh of relief.

This was an oasis, he realized. Needle-leaved palo verdes, mingled with cottonwoods and with yucca and aloe and a sprinkling of wildflowers underneath, grew around the buildings, and he saw a one of the *bandidos* drawing a bucket from a well. Something had to have cut these canyons. Something which had gone underground—a river. Strange to find it in the middle of such rough country.

Stranger still was what flew over the entrance of the main building: a Confederate flag.

A boy, about twelve or thirteen years old, emerged from the hacienda. He trotted over to Slocum and wordlessly helped him to his feet, then stood beside him, propping him up as he wavered on bound ankles. Slocum was about to ask the boy the name of this place, when a tall man, middle-aged and mutton-chopped, emerged from the building, followed by a shorter, but very fat, bald man.

Daddy Jim, thought Slocum, *in the flesh*.

The taller of the two said, "Well, well." He was American, all right, and he wore a Confederate uniform. A general's uniform. "Mr. Slocum, I assume?"

Slocum thought fast. If old Pete was here, Maddie and that idiot Frank were too. Which was how this uniformed fool knew his name. He didn't know what the hell the man was doing in a Reb rig or why the flag was flying, but just to be on the safe side, he stood as tall as he could, and announced, "That's Captain

Slocum, sir. Captain John Slocum, Confederate States of America, at your service." He raised his bound hands. "Sorry not to salute, sir."

The general regarded him for a moment. Slocum noticed a thin scar that ran the length of his cheek. Daddy Jim turned his head and whispered something to the general, and then the general said, "Pablito, my lad, untie our guest."

The boy started to work on his hands.

"I hope you don't mind my asking, Captain," the general continued, the creamy tones of his accent marking him as a Georgia native, most likely, "but where did you receive your captaincy?"

"Under General Sterling Price, sir," Slocum answered automatically.

"Ah, yes. Price," the general said. "A sickly man. Frail, but capable."

Slocum was nobody's fool. He said, "Begging the general's pardon, but it took about a day to walk around him. Had to ride in a wagon pulled by four mules." He pointed to Daddy Jim. "Reckon he was almost the size of your friend there. No offense meant, of course."

Daddy Jim smiled, and the general said, "Yes. Yes, I suppose he was. My men have seen fit to disarm you. I hope *you'll* take no offense."

The boy was finished with his hands, and Slocum rubbed at his wrists while the lad knelt to work at the rope on his ankles. "None taken," Slocum said. "I'm afraid you have the advantage of me. Who might I have the pleasure of addressing?"

The fat man spoke for the first time. "This," he said, pointing a chubby finger, "is General Newton S. Turnbull, C.S.A., Reformed. And I am James O'Hara."

He stepped from beneath the patio's overhang, the sun glistening on his bald head. "My sweet little Maddie told me how you rescued her in the wasteland. I am grateful, sir, truly grateful. I also offer my gravest apologies for the theft of your fine mount, but Colonel Osborn does go off half-cocked sometimes. He's yours, of course." He smiled. "The horse, that is. Not Frank."

Colonel Osborn? The boy finally pulled the ropes free of Slocum's legs, and he gratefully spread them a foot apart, rocking slightly. He tried to picture old Frank in the uniform of a Confederate colonel, and couldn't.

Slocum said, "Then I'll be going. I assume your boys'll give me back my guns?"

General Turnbull frowned and opened his mouth, but Daddy Jim beat him to it. He smiled broadly. "Why, certainly!" he said. "Certainly! But it's getting toward sunset, and you don't want to be traveling the canyons in the dark. Dangerous places, these canyons. Full of snakes and bandits." He held out his hand, motioning Slocum toward him. "Come on up, my boy, and relax. Surely the last part of your journey couldn't have been that comfortable. These Mexicans don't understand that a Southern gentleman is, well, a Southern gentleman. Stay for dinner, a hero's dinner!"

Slocum didn't see that he had much choice.

Candles lined the table and sideboards, lighting the sparsely furnished but enormous room in a festive manner.

The heavy Spanish table was loaded with eclectic fare. A roast suckling pig was the centerpiece—or had been, before it was descended upon and picked clean. Dishes, scraped clean of mashed yams and pickled beets, sat side by side with pans where fat cheese and onion enchiladas had nestled. Pillaged bowls of grits and squash and peas filled spaces between bowls that held the last remnants of crumbled goat cheese and refried beans and Spanish rice, and platters that held the last few blue corn tortillas.

Besides Slocum and Daddy Jim and a mustachioed Mexican *pistolero*, who stuffed his pockmarked face with enough food for three, all the other men at the table—ten of them— were in full dress Confederate uniforms.

General Turnbull sat at the head of the table in a heavy, high-backed Spanish chair, and Maddie O'Hara sat at the foot, picking at her food, avoiding Slocum's glances. Her chair matched the general's—matched all their chairs, for that matter—and she looked lost and frail in its immenseness.

She'd changed her stained and torn dress for the clothes of a Mexican peasant, and wore a white blouse that floated low on her shoulders and showed plenty of cleavage, and a bright skirt. He wasn't sure what color—he'd only caught a glimpse when she'd entered the room and sat down.

Frank eyed him warily—when he could focus, that is—from across the table. He'd made a formal apology for "borrowing" the stud, at Daddy Jim's behest. But Slocum knew that was all it had been, just words to keep the old man happy. Slocum had accepted it, though, and shook Frank's limp and sweaty hand.

"My dear?" Daddy Jim was saying to Maddie. "I'm sure you'll want to rest for the big day tomorrow. If you'll excuse us?"

All the men at the table rose, and Slocum rose with them.

Maddie stood up. As docile as a housecat moving from pillow to pillow on the hearth, she said, "I'll leave you then, gentlemen. It was a lovely meal. Good evening."

She swept out of the room without one look at Slocum. He got a glimpse of her skirt, though. It was red, mostly. Red and orange and purple.

Something was wrong. Something beyond the obvious, something that he hadn't figured out, something to do with Daddy Jim and

Maddie. For a girl who had wanted to get to James O'Hara badly enough to try to kill both Slocum and his horse in the process, she didn't seem any too overjoyed to be in her daddy's company.

And then there was Daddy Jim himself. The man seemed annoyingly familiar, but Slocum couldn't place him.

Turnbull sat down first. They all followed suit. Orderlies—at least, Slocum figured they were orderlies—made fast work of clearing the table, brought out boxes of cigars, brandy snifters, and brandy in crystal decanters, then discreetly disappeared. Slocum accepted a cigar and cut off the end, running it slowly under his nose, savoring it before lighting it. The finest Havana, rolled in the sweat of a Cuban girl's thigh.

What was Turnbull up to, and where was he getting his money? Slocum had a sneaking suspicion that was Daddy Jim's department, but said nothing. He struck a lucifer and held it to the end of his cigar, watching the end glow red as he puffed.

"How's the cigar, Captain?" It was Turnbull himself.

"I was just admiring the flavor, General. This is quite a place you've got here. You boys set on seeing the South rise again?"

Turnbull's eye ticked twice, and a frown flickered over his face. Then he smiled. "Actually, yes. In a way. I hope you don't mind,

Captain, but would you care to tell us a little about your service in the Great War of Secession?"

Slocum rolled the ash off his Havana. "General, if it's all the same to you, I don't care to speak about it. Don't take me wrong. I'm sure y'all have got stories aplenty about fighting for the Glory of the South. But I lost my whole family to it, one way or another."

He raised the snifter and thoughtfully took a sip. It was good brandy. "No, sir, I'd rather not talk about the details, if you don't mind."

Across the table, Frank, in his perfect uniform, managed to hold his eyes steady long enough to glare at him. "Why, I'd think if you really were a son of the South, you'd be proud to tell us! Proud!"

Slocum looked at the younger man. He'd seen dozens like him, full of brave words and the fire to start a fight, but not the courage to see it through. Frank might be able to pick up a scalding-hot coffeepot bare-handed, but he was a coward. Slocum had known that from the first.

Slocum leaned back. He said, "And what did you do in the War, Frank? Besides wait while your mama changed your diapers, that is?"

Laughter burst from most of the company, but Frank stood up, his face red. "You'll call me Colonel. And take that back."

Slocum studied the situation. No one in the

room was armed, so Frank couldn't shoot him in a fit of anger. He chanced a glance at General Turnbull. He was sitting back in his chair, an amused expression on his face. Good.

Slocum said, "Well now, Frank, I don't believe I can do that. First off, it's the truth. Second, I only take back what's been stolen from me. My horse, for instance. That remark, such as it was, was a gift."

Laughter changed to shouts as Frank launched himself across the table, brandy snifters flying, and reached for Slocum's throat. But Slocum was ready for him. He slid easily to one side, jumped up, and pinned Frank's shoulders to the tabletop.

As Frank struggled beneath his arm, Slocum turned toward the general. "I'm right sorry about this, sir," he said calmly, using his other arm to hold Frank's head down. "I'm afraid that Frank, here, has spilled good brandy all over your tablecloth."

If Turnbull had had any doubts before, it looked to Slocum as if he'd dispelled them. Smiling, the general said, "Colonel Osborn!"

Frank went still.

"Colonel, that will be enough. Captain Slocum, you may release him."

Slocum eased his grip, and Frank slithered back across the table, his pristine uniform now blotched and stained with brandy. He ran shaking fingers through his mussed hair, his eyes wobbling in their sockets.

Without so much as another look at Slocum, he said, "Permission to leave, sir?"

The general said, "Granted."

Frank left, slamming the door behind him. An orderly was called to change the tablecloth and pick up the broken glass. The two men closest to Slocum, a young lieutenant and the *pistolero,* slapped him on the back.

Daddy Jim said, "General, our young friend the colonel seems to have raised some doubts as to Captain Slocum's veracity. I'd like to put those doubts to rest."

Turnbull puffed on his cigar. "How so, O'Hara?"

"I myself rode with Captain Slocum for a short time during the conflict."

Slocum's eyes narrowed. O'Hara did seem familiar, but he didn't see how he could have mounted a horse, let alone ridden it into battle. "Beg pardon, sir, but I can't seem to get you placed," Slocum said.

O'Hara laughed, just a quick bubble. "I believe I'll just let that mystery fester, Slocum." He turned to General Turnbull. "For the time being, Captain Slocum is our guest. Our honored guest. Isn't that right, General?"

Turnbull said, "Certainly, certainly," and then changed the subject to horses.

What was going on with these grown-up, masquerading fools?

And what part did Maddie play in it?

10

He was shown to his quarters.

Sparse but comfortable, the room was in the main hacienda, toward the back. From his window, he could see that the camp was quite a bit larger than he'd first thought. What looked like an enormous kitchen garden, complete with scarecrows, and adjoining fields of crops ran back into the murky distance to his right. Eight more barracks were to the rear of this building, narrow ends toward him, the lanterns inside each throwing a soft wash of light over the building next to it.

He saw men lingering on the porches of two of the barracks. White men in uniform, although not nearly so formal as the uniforms at dinner. These boys were slouched on the stoops in their shirtsleeves, suspenders dangling, as they talked softly. Somewhere, someone was playing "Old Black Joe" on a mouth harp.

If all the barracks were full, Slocum figured that there were probably at least two hundred men in this hidden canyon, not counting the Mexicans or the officers.

Not very many if you planned to start a war. Quite a few if you only wanted to start trouble.

His attention turned to the canyon walls, spread widely and towering. He had to watch them quite a while, but he spotted three sentries, little more than tiny black shapes in the distance: rising, moving, ducking out of sight again. If he'd seen three, just from his window's narrow view, there were more.

The hacienda was built to withstand a siege. The roof wasn't flat, like the other buildings in the complex, but canted, and topped with red clay tiles. The front door was heavy oak, several inches thick, with strategically placed gun ports. The walls were adobe, three feet thick—looking out the window was like looking out through a tunnel—and the gun-ported shutters were on the inside.

Additionally, there was an iron band, three inches wide, that spanned the top of each window—at least his window, and the windows in the dining room—about five inches from the inside. A groove down each side and a deep well across the bottom led him to believe that it was some kind of metal fortification, one that would drop down like a guillotine to keep out intruders.

Or perhaps, keep them from getting out.

The presence of two heavy metal rings above the window—and two holes just below it, outside the frame—told him that if he wanted to find out just what kind of fortification it was, all he had to do was pull the rings. And all he had to do to lock it down was shove them—and the rods that they were most certainly attached to—into the lower holes.

He didn't want to find out that badly.

Blowing out the already dim lantern, Slocum stretched out on the bed and folded his hands behind his head, elbows cocked out. He'd been trying to recall Daddy Jim O'Hara from his war days, but so far, had had no luck. He'd tried picturing him younger, imagining him with hair, then a mustache, then a beard, but nothing clicked.

And what was Turnbull's story? The man was a lunatic—they were all lunatics, if they thought they were going to start the Civil War again with two hundred men, and in Arizona of all places!

So what was the point? What were they really after? Why the *bandidos*?

The door creaked. Slocum reached for his gun, remembering just as his fingers touched air that it was most likely riding the hip of a Mexican bandit.

"Slocum?" A whisper in the dark.

He relaxed. It was Maddie. Maybe now he'd get some answers.

"Slocum, are you in here?"

He could see her now, through the murk. He said, "I'm here."

She slipped in the door, closing it quietly behind her. "Where are you?" she whispered.

He leaned over and lit the lamp, keeping the wick turned low.

She was dressed in a man's robe, green silk, one of Daddy Jim's by the way she swam in it. She kept picking at the sleeves nervously, pulling them up to free her hands, and they kept falling down just as fast as she pushed them up.

"Slocum," she began, "I . . . we . . . that is, they . . ."

She kept pushing at the sleeves.

Slocum sat up and swung his feet to the floor, propping his elbows on his knees. "Maddie," he said softly, trying to sound reassuring, lest she replay that little scene on the desert and go loco on him again. "Are you in over your head?"

She looked relieved. And terrified. The masks she'd worn on the desert and at dinner had slipped away, and she suddenly looked like a scared little girl running to Daddy for comfort. Although she hadn't gone to her daddy's room. She'd come to his.

"Oh, Jesus, yes," she breathed. "Slocum, you wouldn't believe, I mean . . ."

"Maddie, sit down." He patted the empty stretch of bed beside him. "Sit down and start from the beginning."

She sat, still plucking at the robe. "I . . . I don't know where the beginning is."

"Then start at the middle. Start anywhere."

She took a deep breath, and then she began. "Daddy Jim's gold, for instance. I don't think it was ever going to the smelter at Caballo Loco. I think it was supposed to come here all along. And it's not the first time either."

A green sleeve slithered down her arm. She pushed it back up. "That's the sixth shipment since I came to Arizona to stay with Daddy Jim. And that's another thing. Slocum, do people get cured from consumption? From tuberculosis?"

That was a hell of a thing to ask him. But he figured he'd best play along and keep her happy. He said, "I don't know. They get better, maybe. After a long time."

When she didn't say anything, he offered, "Dry air's good for the lungs."

She didn't look at him. She stared straight ahead at the wall, her lips pursed, her jaw working. She said, "Well, if they get cured, can they do it in six months?"

"I don't think so. Can we get back to what the Sam Hill is going on with these yahoos? What are they using the gold for? What are they *doing* out here?"

She shrugged, and the robe sagged again. "I probably never had it." Her eyes were still focused on the wall. Absently, she plucked at her sleeves. "I probably never had it at all. I told Felicity it was just a touch of the ague, but no, she sent me to that doctor, and then

Daddy Jim drops out of the clear blue sky and—''

Slocum put his hand on her wrist, as much to stop her fiddling with the robe as to quiet her. ''What the hell are you talking about?''

At last she turned her face toward him. ''Nothing,'' she said. ''Nothing of consequence anyway. Nothing to do with you.''

He found he couldn't take his eyes from hers. He heard himself say, ''Maddie, what's going on?''

He meant the way he was feeling at that moment, wondering why a certified she-devil would get him all itchy and make his prick swell in his britches, but she chose to take it the other way.

''They all stop talking when I come into a room,'' she said quietly, eye-to-eye, as if she couldn't look away from his face either. ''They treat Daddy Jim like a prince. I knew he could talk a snake into sprouting feathers, but . . . And when we ran into the *bandidos,* I was scared, but Frank acted like he knew them. He *did* know them. They blindfolded me. I don't know where we are. But they have more than two hundred men here, and they're waiting for something.''

She began to speak faster, all in a whispery rush. ''Frank's . . . well, he's different than I thought. Daddy Jim's not the same either. I'm supposed to be married tomorrow, to Frank. I told Daddy Jim I'd changed my mind, and he got angry—I've never seen him get so fired up—and said that I ought to be grateful to marry a fine, upstanding officer like Frank Osborn, considering Chicago and all, and that I was going to marry him whether I liked it or not, so I shut up and said 'Yes, Daddy.' And I'm ashamed of myself. And I'm sorry about how I was out on the desert, Slocum, the way I acted, I mean. I'm not a bitch, really, and I'm not prissy, or . . . It's just that I . . . I . . ."

He thought he was going to get an explanation, but after a pause, she just said, "I—I'm sorry. But you came for your horse, I knew you'd come for your horse, I gave him water . . ."

And then she was crying, and he took her into his arms, comforting her, although he was damned if he'd understood half of what she'd said. He still didn't know what was going on with the glorious "Confederate Army, Reformed." And what was all that horseshit about tuberculosis and Chicago?

"Shhh, Maddie, shhh," he whispered as she sobbed into his shoulder. She was really crying this time. He rubbed her back, the silk slippery beneath his fingers, slippery on her skin, and it didn't take a second for him to realize she was naked beneath it. He knew it as soon as he touched her.

It should have been the last thing on his mind, considering the mess he was in. It should have been the last thing on her mind too, considering that come tomorrow she was supposed to marry good old Frank, the goggle-eyed horse thief. But before he knew it, he was sliding that enormous silk robe from her shoulders, and she was helping him.

"Maddie, are you sure?" he said between kisses, his hands full of ripe breasts, his cock engorged and pounding.

"Yes," she sighed, her eyes damp with tears, kissing him again before she went to work at his belt buckle, then the buttons on his pants.

"Oh, yes," she breathed again as he sprang free and she wrapped both hands around him. "Do me hard, Slocum," she whispered. "Do me rough and fast. There'll be time for slow later on."

"Anything for a lady," he said, just before his mouth closed on one tight nipple, just before she straddled him and sank down on his cock.

The fit was tight enough that she gasped loudly, throwing her head back and exposing her throat, but she was already primed inside, so slippery that he felt her juices drenching his balls as she enveloped him.

He grabbed her around the waist and without breaking contact, flipped her on her back, on the bed. Propping himself up at arm's length, he began to thrust into her, burying himself to the hilt, pulling out almost all the way, then ramming home again, over and over.

Beneath him, she gripped both sides of the bed, clutching at the blankets, bracing herself against the power of those thrusts, her breasts swaying with the concussion of each stroke, her channel growing still wetter, slipperier.

She tugged and squeezed at him with her internal muscles, lifting her hips to meet him, and all the time whispering, "Yes," and "Harder," and "God, yes," and finally, a long hissed-out "Sssslocum!" just before the climax took her.

He paused, dropping down to brace himself on his elbows as she quaked. He licked the sweat from her face, liked the taste, and continued down her throat. He had just reached her collarbones when she whispered, in a throaty growl, "Again."

He lifted his face and smiled. "Honey, I've barely started."

He began to move within her slowly; long, easy strokes that soon had her begging for him to end it. She struggled beneath him, trying to put herself on top where she could control the proceedings, but he was having none of it. He kept up that slow pace, sometimes pausing between strokes, holding himself back, holding off his climax, listening as Maddie's whispered, feverish pleas turned to shudders.

Finally, he couldn't hold it in check any longer. He began to drive into her, hard. Maddie's eyes grew big and she let out a cry just before the world turned upside down and the seed erupted from him.

She came again, with him this time, and they both lay there in a tangle of arms and legs, shaking and panting.

After a moment, Slocum slowly raised his head to look at her. She had a dazed look, her head turned to the side, her eyes unfocused.

He whispered, "Maddie?"

She turned toward him. She stared at him for a minute, lifting her hand to brush back the hair that had fallen over his brow, smoothing it.

"My God, Slocum," she said at last, languorously, her expression dead serious. "How much better will you be once you've got your clothes off?"

It took him a second to realize that he still had his shirt on, and his pants were puddled around his knees. He laughed, and she put her fingers over his mouth to hold the noise in.

He kissed her hand, then said, "Give me about twenty minutes, and we'll find out."

"I like that. The sound of you laughing, I mean. Well, the twenty minutes part too."

He rolled off her—and out of her—to her disappointed little "Oh."

"Twenty minutes," he reminded her, smiling and shucking out of his britches, then unbuttoning and pulling off his shirt. He'd sweated through it. He tossed the shirt to one side and lifted his arm to put it around Maddie, but she'd already risen and gone to the window.

Standing there, nude in the frail light, she reminded him of nothing so much as one of those Italian paintings—"Venus by Lamplight" or something. Long dark hair trailed halfway down her back and led his gaze to a glorious backside, the cheeks dimpled and round. Her legs were long and slender, but not too slender. He was just coming back up to her fanny again when she turned around, presenting him with a whole new garden of delights to contemplate.

His cock stirred, and he was just about to tell her to come back to bed, that he'd overestimated when he'd said twenty minutes, when she said, "They're going to attack Tucson."

11

"What?" Slocum sounded like he didn't believe her.

"I said, they're going to attack Tucson. I think. I was listening through the door." Maddie lifted her head, shook back the hair that sweat had stuck to her skin. "I don't think it's any time soon. Daddy Jim's leaving for more gold come Saturday. He's leaving me here," she added. "Leaving me behind. With Frank." She made a face. "Oh, joy."

Slocum sat up and swung his legs to the floor. He was prettier naked than he had been in clothes, she thought, and that was saying something. She would have liked to spend a week locked in a hotel room with him, maybe two weeks, naked and sweaty and rutting like there was no tomorrow, stopping only for sleep or room service or to explore a new scar on that handsome, weathered body. But there *was* a tomorrow. It was her wedding day.

"You're crazy," he said, leaning over to pick up her robe. A green silk pool on the floor. "There's a garrison at Tucson."

She stiffened. "Don't call me crazy."

113

He paused for a second to look at her, then said, "I'm sorry, Maddie. You're not crazy. I've seen crazy, and you're not it. Tell me what you heard."

"Daddy Jim was talking to that General Turnstile or Turnover or whatever his name is."

"Turnbull." Slocum brought the robe up and put it on the bed beside him.

"Well, when I knew him, he was plain Bob Turner from Wichita. He doesn't remember me now. At least, he didn't give any sign."

Slocum opened his mouth, but she said, "Before you ask, I knew him from Chicago. I was a whore, all right? I'm not proud of it, but I'm not ashamed either. I wasn't just any whore, but a fifty-dollar one—a hundred for the whole night—and fantasy was my specialty. You know, Little Bo Peep or the French Maid or the Tiger Lady? Like that."

Slocum nodded dumbly, as if he was trying to imagine her dressed in frills with a bonnet and a staff and a sheep. Men.

"Bob Turner's—or General Turnbull's—fantasy was to have me wear a hoop skirt and tie him up and call him 'nigger,' and whip him before we got down to it. He only came the one night, but I remember him. It took two weeks for the bruises to go away. I suppose when you beat up a lot of whores, their faces tend to run together."

Slocum was just sitting there, hands on his

knees. She said, "Well, aren't you going to say how shocked you are? Make a rude comment? Try to save me? Something?"

Slocum looked up. "I'm not shocked. Well, sort of, but not the way you think. Do you know any of the others?"

"What's that supposed to mean?"

"Just what it sounded like. Don't go reading in what I didn't say."

She studied his face. "I'm sorry. No. I didn't recognize anybody else."

Smiling, he tossed the robe to her one-handed. "Put that on while we're talking, honey, or I'm going to drool all over myself. Bo Peep?"

He winked at her, and she grinned in spite of herself. She'd needed comforting, needed closeness, and a relatively safe male presence, and he was the only person within two hundred miles to fit the bill. Now she realized that he wasn't a bad character, not really. She'd been right to take a chance on him. He was, in fact, a kind man.

She never wanted to be on his bad side again, though. She reminded herself there was something dangerous bubbling under Slocum's surface, something a lot worse than dumping women off horses. Something she didn't want to see.

She shrugged into the robe and wrapped it around her. "Anyway, Daddy Jim told the general that it wasn't dried up yet, that there was plenty more where that came from. I'm pretty sure he meant the gold. And then the general said that once they took Tucson and it started, they'd need all that Daddy Jim could get his hands on, and Daddy Jim said not to worry, because after I married Frank that would take care of it."

She went back to the bed and sat beside Slocum, her hand on his bare leg. He was a well-put-together man. "Then somebody came, and I had to leave. I don't know what it means. I can't figure what my marrying Frank has to do with it." She squeezed his knee. "Were you really a captain?"

"A long time ago."

She slid her hand a few inches up his thigh, skimming her fingers over a scar, following the hard line of a muscle. Tomorrow she'd have to marry that pea-brain Frank, unless she could think of a way out of it, and then only God knew what would happen. Tonight was hers, though.

Suddenly, she had a bright thought. "Maybe when they attack Tucson, Frank'll be killed."

Slocum snorted. "They'll all be killed. Bunch of damned lunatics."

"Slocum?" She slid her hand all the way up his leg, then curled her fingers around his prick, smiling when it swelled in her grasp. With her free hand, she reached into the deep pocket of her robe and found the bit of soft cord she'd brought. Deftly, she looped it around his shaft, behind his balls, and tied it off loosely. By the time she finished, his erection had swollen to take up the slack.

"Maddie?" Slocum had a curious smile on his face. "What the devil are you doing?"

She stood up and let her robe fall to the floor. "That's the Maddie Sewell makeshift cock ring. That's my real name, Maddie Sewell." She bent slightly, swinging a breast just above his lips. On the second pass, he caught the tip in his teeth. "It'll make things . . . better for you," she hissed, as both her nipples puckered and tightened and she felt the release of moisture between her legs.

Slocum let go of her breast to say, "Don't see how that's possible, Maddie." He cupped his hands over her breasts, then ran them down her sides and to her fanny, kneading it gently before he slipped his hand down and up, and began to stroke her.

"Bo Peep, eh?" he said, grinning.

"Oh, Slocum," she breathed. She bent lower, her elbows on Slocum's shoulders, her eyes closing. "Why didn't I meet you first?"

A tongue circled her left nipple, then teased at the other before he sucked it deep into his mouth. His hand just kept moving, stroking, petting her, sending prickling ripples, then waves, of pleasure up her spine.

She felt him moving her then, and she followed, eyes closed, trusting, as he brought her forward and eased her down upon him.

Just the head first. His open hand bracing her fanny wouldn't let her go any further. She rode the first three inches, wanting more, wanting it all, until finally, he leaned back and slowly let her down. He was huge this time, so huge that it was almost painful.

But she rode him, his hands touching her belly, her breasts, feathering over her nipples or her arms or touching her between her legs, where that big cock slid in and out of her. She knew he was watching it—she wished she could see too—and then she felt herself rising, rising, and suddenly the climax overtook her, lifting her up and out of herself. Her brain went blank and void, as if there were no room left in it for anything but sensation.

She must have cried out, for she felt Slocum's hand cover her mouth as wave after wave took her, shattered her. And then she was sprawled on Slocum's chest, their sweat-slick bodies panting to the same rhythm, and Slocum was groping between her legs—his legs—for the string. At last he found the knot and pulled it free, breathing a hoarse, "Jesus, Maddie, are you trying to drive me crazy?"

"Yes, Slocum," she panted, grinning. "Tell me, is it working?"

He threw the sodden cord to the floor, then flipped her over onto her back, his cock still hard and thumping inside her, filling her in the most pleasant way possible.

He smiled. "How 'bout I show you, Miss Bo Peep?"

Maddie brushed through her hair a last time and tied it back with a ribbon, then walked down the hall, and into the big dining room. It was nine-thirty in the morning, and everybody had long since eaten and started marching up and down or throwing around orders, or whatever it was that they did.

She thought about going to the kitchen and asking Maria for a cup of coffee, but decided against it. She wanted to find Frank first. She had a few questions to ask him.

Daddy Jim was on the porch, twiddling a cigar that had gone out. She bent and hugged him.

He grinned up at her. "Mornin', sugar pie. All ready for the big event?"

Actually, she wasn't ready for the wedding, not one to Frank anyway, but she knew better than to get Daddy Jim riled again. She smiled and said, "Of course, Daddy. How was breakfast?" He liked to talk about food. It would distract him.

He fell right into it. "Marvelous!" he said, a blissful expression lighting his face. "Eggs Benedict! Maria must have used every egg on the place. And then some lovely country fried potatoes—just the way I like them, with a tad of onion and bacon, and with those crispy little edges. Not quite like the way you make them, Maddie, but fine, very fine. And then there were the sausages. . . ."

She let him go on about breakfast for a few minutes, and then she said, "Daddy Jim? Do you know where Frank is?"

He pursed his lips. "I believe I just saw him go in the officers barracks." He smiled. "You sure you want to see him on your wedding day? Bad luck, they say."

"Oh, Daddy! You? Superstitious?" She lit his cigar and he laughed. Then she stood up, kissed his bald head, and started across the courtyard, to the officers quarters.

She wasn't walking too well. Lord, but Slocum was big! She'd gone two years without a man, but Slocum had more than made up for it. She found herself thinking that she hoped no one would ask her to ride a horse for the next day or two, and then, in spite of what she was about to do, she smiled. They'd had a good time last night. No, good didn't cover it, not by half. It had felt wonderful to be in a man's arms again, to let him take control: to *trust* him to take control.

She couldn't see herself trusting Frank any farther than she could throw him. Maybe not that far.

Too many things were wrong. Either Frank explained himself, or she'd go to Daddy Jim. And she wouldn't fall back into some convenient role. Not the dutiful daughter, not the compliant fiancée or the submissive wife. This time she'd be just Maddie. Well, as much of Maddie as she knew how to be.

She reached the barracks. The door was open, and she stuck her head inside. "Frank?"

He was alone. He stepped from the shadows at the other end and walked toward her, past the cots and bunk beds, smiling. "Maddie!" Light from the windows painted him bright every third step. "Are you sure you should be down here, sweetheart? After all, the wedding's tonight."

He reached her and took her hand, but she jerked it away. Immediately his expression changed from joy to annoyance. "Oh. Going to be that way, are you? What do you want?"

"Answers."

"To what? Listen, Maddie, I don't have time for—"

Best to just jump in with both feet. If she was wrong, he could prove it to her. She said, "I want to know why you stole Daddy Jim's gold."

His eyes did that little dance again. "*What?*"

"You heard me." She kept her voice flat, her arms folded over her chest. "I want to know what in the world possessed you to hire those men. They killed our guards—men I knew. Men I *liked*, Frank."

"Oh, really?" he sneered, his voice like a snotty little boy's. "And just how well did you 'like' them, Maddie?"

She slapped his cheek, hard. When he

turned to face her, blood seeped from one nostril. He fished in his pocket and pulled out a handkerchief. Daubing at his nose, then looking at the blood with disdain, he said, "You liked them that well, did you? I know all about Chicago, you know."

That took her by surprise, but this time she had herself a little more under control, and she didn't hit him. Instead, she said, "Frank, changing the subject won't work. Making insinuations won't work. I know you did it. Oh, you can make half-assed excuses all you want. 'Somebody else named Frank Osborn was thrown off a horse,' " she said, in a biting imitation of him. "Really, Frank! Did you think anybody'd believe you wouldn't even try looking for me in Halcyon, not if you'd been on the up-and-up? I have to give you one thing, though. When you came up on us, on the desert? That was real good acting, Frank. You never gave a hint that those were your men Slocum buried. Or that it was your gold—for the moment anyway—that was missing. You should have gone on the stage. You missed your calling."

Frank stared at her for a moment, one corner of his mouth twitching. She didn't know whether he would hit her or throttle her or make love to her. None of them was a prospect she relished. She was about to take a step back when he said, "I did it for us, Maddie."

She hadn't expected an admission, at least

not right off the bat. And that he'd done it for them? If he imagined for one second that she'd believe him, he was crazier than she thought he was. But she repeated, "You did it for us."

"Sure! Sure, I did!" His voice had changed tenor, gone all creamy. "Do you have any idea how much gold he's shipped down here in the last few years? Payrolls, putting up these buildings, those goddamn *bandidos*—he's paid for everything. And do you have any idea how much money you have to pay a *bandido* to keep him from robbing you?"

She imagined it was quite a lot. She imagined, in fact, that the *bandidos* were just waiting for a chance to rob them—not just that measly fifteen thousand, but the whole pie. The one who'd been at dinner last night, that Montoya, gave her the creeps. When the others weren't looking, he fairly raped her with his eyes.

She said, "And how was I to figure into this?" She couldn't wait for this one.

Frank didn't disappoint her. Eyes flicking to the side, then back again, he said, "I was going to come for you in Halcyon. And we'd get married, and then we'd go back to the ranch, and—"

"How could we go back to the ranch, Frank? Daddy Jim would have shot you on sight."

· Frank sighed, and twisted his head to the left—and back again—for no apparent reason. "Because he was supposed to—now, don't get mad, honey lamb—he was supposed to be dead."

In spite of herself, she felt her brows shoot up. "Dead?"

Frank took her by the shoulders. "Maddie, he's just using you. He's just using you to get the ranch. Our ranch."

Who was using whom? Frank was playing her for a sucker, all right.

"Sewell, that's your name," he continued. "That ranch was owned by Horace Sewell. Your father."

She spoke very slowly, as if to an insane person, because she was now firmly convinced he was just that. "Frank, my father died from cholera when I was just a baby. My mother told me so."

He shook his head. Slow at first, then convulsively. "No, Maddie. No, no, no. Maybe that's what she wanted you to think, but no. Why else do you think that Jim would hire detectives to find you? Why else would he go all the way to Chicago and pay that woman you worked for five thousand dollars to con you into leaving? Because legally, you hold title to that land. The land that's financing all this."

Her knees felt shaky. This part was the truth, she felt it. She whispered, "I never had consumption? He *paid* Felicity?"

He put his arms around her, idly picking at

an invisible something on her sleeve, and she was too weak to stop him.

Felicity had lied. Frank had lied. Daddy Jim had lied. The only one in the world who hadn't lied to her was Slocum.

She felt Frank stroking her hair, hunting through it. "Oh, honey," he whispered, "we could have the best time. Do you have lice? They hide everywhere, you know."

Maddie started to jerk away but he held on tighter. "Think of it! Tens of thousands, maybe hundreds of thousands, still in the ground. And it could be ours, all ours. We can still have it."

His fingers in her hair felt like snakes, the touch of ten reptiles. She shoved him away. "You are scum. You are *crazy* scum!"

"What?" Frank had the nerve to appear shocked.

"Lies. All lies. Except the part about the robbery. That I believe. I believe you were going to kill Daddy Jim, and probably me too. Poor, sweet, dear Daddy Jim, who's only been kind to me." She said it, although the words were bitter in her mouth. "Shame on you, Frank Osborn. I hope you rot in Hell."

She turned and ran from the building, on her way to tell Daddy Jim, on her way to tell one liar about another.

12

He woke at about ten in the morning.

Maddie was gone, but she'd forgotten the cord. He picked it up from the floor and rolled it in his hand, smiling. A fellow learned something new every day.

He poured out water from the pitcher that had been left on his bureau the night before. He splashed his face over the bowl, then picked up the shaving brush, dunked it, and began to scrub it over a cake of soap. Through the window came the sounds of drilling troops outside, troops chanting a litany as they marched.

A chill ran through him despite the warm morning. All he wanted was to get his horse and get the hell away from here.

And maybe take Maddie with him.

A half hour later, shaved and dressed, Slocum found his way to the dining room. No breakfast was in evidence—no people either, for that matter—but through the window, he caught a glimpse of Daddy Jim's bald head.

He found him on the porch, creaking back and forth in a king-sized rocking chair, smok-

ing a cigar. "Fine morning, isn't it, Captain?"
he said when Slocum came out. He kept on
rocking.

"I expect so, if your taste runs to hot and
sweaty." From the front porch, Slocum could
see one troop drilling in the distance, out past
the sage on the far side of the corrals. "Don't
suppose I could find a cup of coffee around
here? Like to see to my horse too."

"Your horse has already been cared for.
That appaloosa made quite a hit with the *bandidos*. He's already covered three mares.
Randy son of a buck, isn't he?" Daddy Jim
smiled up at him, but there was something behind that smile, something secret and un-
wholesome.

Slocum said, "I reckon."

Daddy Jim twisted his head toward the
door. "Pablito!" he bellowed.

In no time at all, the young boy who had
cut Slocum's ropes yesterday appeared at the
door. "Señor O'Hara?"

"Bring the captain here a cup of coffee. And
some breakfast, if there's any left."

The boy scurried away, and O'Hara continued. "You missed breakfast by about four
hours. We rise early here in camp. Drill during
the cooler hours, you see. I'm afraid General
Turnbull considers you a slugabed. But then,
Maddie slept in late too. Ah, that was fast, Pablito!"

The boy set a covered tray upon a small table to the left of Daddy Jim, and whisked away the cloth. Coffee, a few hard rolls, jam.

"Sit down, Captain, sit down!" Daddy Jim gestured toward a vacant chair. "Sorry we couldn't do better, but we'll take luncheon in about an hour."

Slocum nodded his thanks to the boy, then sat down and slathered strawberry jam on a roll. He ate half of the first one—it was good jam—before he said, "Mr. O'Hara, I've been tryin' like the devil to place you. You said you knew me?"

O'Hara chuckled. "Call me Daddy. Or call me Jim. Would it be of any help to you if I told you we met during the Western Campaign?" He puffed on his cigar and stared out over the compound, surveying it as if he owned the place. Which he probably did, if Slocum didn't miss his guess. "You served with William Quantrill, and quite ably. I myself was with Bill Anderson."

Bloody Bill Anderson. Quantrill had been bad enough, and Slocum wasn't proud he'd ridden with him. But Bloody Bill had been three times as bad. He and his men had fought through every campaign like mad dogs, and they took souvenirs.

Scalps. Fingers. Testicles.

Slocum didn't give any sign, though. He chewed on the last half of his roll thoughtfully, then washed it down with Pablito's excellent coffee. "Nope," he said, swallowing. " 'Fraid I can't place you."

O'Hara chuckled. "Small wonder. I was a much different man then."

Before Slocum could respond, O'Hara said, "Ah. Here comes the fair Maddie. Hotly pursued too."

Maddie marched across the compound, fists curled at the ends of swinging arms, a determined look on her face. Frank was beside her, talking quickly, angrily. He grabbed her arm and pulled her back, and she hauled off and slugged him in the jaw.

Frank went halfway down as Slocum stifled a laugh, but he came up again and grabbed Maddie by her skirts, pulling her back.

"Lovers' spat," said Daddy Jim O'Hara.

"She's got a punch," said Slocum, rubbing his own jaw, and something went through his head, something about how it was bad luck for the groom to see the bride on the wedding day.

O'Hara laughed. "You sound like you've been at the wrong end of . . . Say, Frank's getting a little rough with my little flower, don't you think?"

Slocum didn't respond, because he was already jumping off the porch. Frank slapped Maddie—twice, and hard—before Slocum plowed into him, knocking him to the ground.

Frank landed, sputtering, in the dust. Maddie cried, "Tell him, Frank! If you don't tell him, I swear to God I will!"

Slocum was about to ask her who Frank was supposed to tell and just what it was he was supposed to say, when Frank leapt up and charged, butting Slocum in the belly with his head. The jolt sailed him back ten feet and he landed on his backside, but he landed mad. Frank threw himself on Slocum then, but Slocum rolled to the side and Frank went flat in the dirt. Before he could roll over, Slocum's knee was in the small of his back, pinning him.

He looked over at Maddie, but she wasn't there. She was already up on the porch, her hands clutched around Daddy Jim's massive arm, her lips rapidly whispering in his ear.

Slocum waited. Despite all the high-ranking riffraff in this hidden canyon, it was Daddy Jim O'Hara who ran the show.

Frank jerked to one side in a feeble last-ditch effort to free himself, but Slocum batted him on the back of the head with an open hand. "Hold still," he growled under his breath. "I'm waitin' on your master's voice."

But O'Hara didn't speak. He waved, a small gesture, and Slocum hauled Frank to his feet, pinning one arm behind his back. "Sorry to get your pretty uniform dirty again, Frank," he said as he pushed him toward James O'Hara.

"You may release him, Captain," O'Hara said when they reached the porch.

Frank flailed back with his fist, a child's motion, but Slocum had already stepped out of the way. He stood to one side, waiting to see what would happen next.

O'Hara opened his mouth to speak, but Frank beat him to it. "It's a lie!" he shouted. "She's lying, I tell you! They're all a bunch of liars."

O'Hara's jovial face slipped for a second into something darker, but then the mask was back in place. If Slocum had blinked, he would have missed it.

"Lies, Frank?" said the fat man cordially.

"Well, it's . . . uh . . ." Frank looked at Maddie, whose face was unreadable, at least to Slocum, and then back at O'Hara.

"Now, Frank." Daddy Jim leaned forward, balancing pudgy elbows on fat knees. "Are you having another episode? Do you need to go back to Denver?"

Frank seemed to shrink in on himself. Episode? Denver? Slocum felt as confused as Maddie suddenly looked.

O'Hara continued. "Frank, Maddie told me you said some crazy things. Terrible things. And then you tried to force yourself on her." He clucked his tongue. "And on the day of your wedding too. Couldn't you wait just seven hours?"

Frank was looking smaller and smaller.

"He shoved me down on a cot, Daddy Jim," she said, sniffing. Her whole presence was different when O'Hara was around. Softer, more helpless. Fragile, almost. Slocum wondered that he didn't have the servants carrying her around in a litter. "He said he'd cut my face if I didn't let him. Oh, Daddy, he was talking crazy, saying terrible things! But I got away. I was so scared!"

Frank looked horrified. "Daddy, I never—"

"Shut up," said O'Hara.

Maddie sank into a chair. She covered her face with her hands and began to sob. Slocum recognized this trick—it was the same one she'd pulled on him that first night. A fine bunch of characters he'd gotten himself mixed up with! He suspected that, after all, he was the only sane one in the whole damn lot.

O'Hara patted Maddie's head, which only served to make her sob louder. As if he were addressing a small boy who had just broken a window, he said, "Frank, I'm going to have to put you under house arrest until I decide what to do with you this time. Needless to say, there'll still be a wedding. Just no wedding night. For the time being anyway. Now, go on."

Frank paused, opened his mouth, then closed it.

"Go on, boy."

Frank said, "Yes, sir," and walked back down to the barracks. The only sign he gave of frustration was to savagely kick a stone out of his way.

"And change into a clean uniform!" O'Hara

called after him. Frank gave no reply.

O'Hara turned toward Slocum, for whom a light had just gone on. Osborn.

"Family squabble," O'Hara said. "Can't be helped." He patted Maddie's head again, and she gasped air for a louder wail.

Slocum said, "I remember you now. Jimmy Ray Osborn. They called you the Butcher of Bent Horn. Frank's your son, isn't he?"

The fat man laughed. "Very good! Excellent, Captain, excellent! You've caught me out. And yes, that heap of hog guts I laughingly call a man is my son. I like to think he takes after his mother. Delicate, temperamental thing she was. Sensitive. Went crazy as a bucket full of eels when Frank was about nine. I have his power of attorney, of course. In and out of insane asylums. They say he's cured, then another relapse. And so on."

And this was the man O'Hara had picked for Maddie? Maybe she really *was* crying behind those hands.

"I sometimes think I should just do with Frank what I did with his mother," O'Hara continued, staring out toward the officers barracks Frank had just disappeared into.

Slocum had to ask. "What was that?"

"Hauled her out behind the smokehouse and shot her, of course." He turned toward Slocum. "But enough about Frank. Captain, would you please convey Maddie to her room? Can't stand a crying woman. And stop by the kitchen on your way back. Find out how much longer till lunch."

Slocum said, "Whatever you say, Jim," and went up on the porch to help Maddie to her feet. While O'Hara re-lit his Havana, Slocum tucked Maddie's narrow shoulders under his arm and slowly started back through the hacienda, with Maddie wailing her heart out and hiccoughing all the way.

They came to her room, and after he'd opened the door and taken her inside, she suddenly straightened and looked up, dry-eyed. As expected.

"That sonofabitch!" was the first thing out of her mouth. "That weaselly, two-bit, raw-butted sonofabitch! Frank is his son, his goddamn *son*! He told me Frank was away on business, not locked up in some asylum! It makes sense now, Slocum. The whole thing makes sense! Steal my gold, will they!"

"What?"

By way of an answer, she suddenly wrapped her arms around Slocum, kissing him with all her might, squeezing his backside and running her hands over his back. He was just starting to enjoy it when she pushed away from him.

"Get out of here," she said, putting her hand in the middle of his chest and shoving him toward the door. "He's waiting. But come back. I need to talk to you, and soon."

Slocum found himself standing alone in the

hallway, waiting for his erection to die. From outside, the Butcher of Bent Horn, who had slashed woman and children to pieces with saber and knife, killed and mutilated and raped his way across Kansas and Missouri, and disappeared without a trace when the war was over, yelled, "Maria! Anybody! Damn it, somebody tell me when we eat!"

13

As it happened, he didn't get back to Maddie's room. Lunch was served, an eclectic extravaganza that ranged from roasted chickens through curried beef, all the way to caramel custard, called *flan*, for desert.

No mention was made of Frank's absence from the table. Slocum knew better than to bring it up, and nobody else did.

After lunch, he tried to go down the hall, but Carlos Montoya, the pockmarked *bandido* chief who'd sat beside him, called him out on the porch.

"I think you would visit your horse sooner, *Capitán*," he said, picking up his guns from the box where all the diners checked their firearms.

"I keep trying," Slocum said, and belched.

The bandit laughed, exposing a gap on one side where his eyetooth was gone. "This food. It is too rich. It gives the burning heart, *sí*?"

Slocum allowed himself a smile. "Reckon it does."

He stepped down off the porch and followed Carlos to the corrals. There was a Mexican in a paddock with old Pete, clipping a lead rope to his halter. Pete's head was up, scenting the air. He whickered.

"What's going on?" Slocum asked.

Montoya smiled. "This spotted horse of yours, he is one fool for the ladies. They bring the black mare to him again. Look."

Sure enough, another *bandido* was just opening the gate. He led in an animated black mare, a *paso* by the looks of her, who pawed the ground nervously and shook her long mane, and immediately swung her rump toward the stud.

The men didn't waste any time. The other Mexican brought Pete forward. He nuzzled the mare until her tail was cocked to the side and she was shifting from hind leg to hind leg and nickering, and then he reared and mounted her.

As the grunting horses coupled, Montoya said, "You would sell this horse, señor?"

Slocum thumbed his hat back. "Seems to me you're gettin' part of him for free right now."

Montoya wasn't looking at him. He only had eyes for the horses. Absently, one hand dropped to his crotch. "He is *muy macho*, this one. This afternoon, maybe, we try the chestnut mare the woman rode. That woman, she is nice too, eh? Sweet, but with a bite, like mesquite honey."

After a time, the appy dismounted, his cock still extended and dripping. While one man led the mare away, the other tied Pete to the rail, brought a bucket of water, and began to slosh the horse down.

Montoya had gotten control of himself, and both arms were now propped on the fence. "You see?" He tipped a hand, pointing to the man working under the appy's belly. "We take good care. Keep him clean. He has the loose shoe, though."

"Don't suppose you've had the time to reset it. Given his busy schedule and all."

The Mexican slapped him on the back and nearly knocked him over. "*Señor Capitán,* you are a funny fellow! Busy schedule!"

Montoya hung around while Slocum reset the shoe, down at the forge. Men in uniform came and went, eyed him warily, but didn't speak. Montoya talked enough for all of them, though.

There were about fifty *bandidos* in all, Slocum learned, only six of which were in camp. The rest, in small groups of six or eight, prowled other entrances to the canyon maze, keeping out unwelcome visitors. And Jim O'Hara paid them well.

"My men do what they would do anyway," said Montoya with a shrug, stroking his mustache. "We take some horses, we take some money. And the *patron* gives us supplies, and pays on top of that, in gold."

"And why didn't they take that fifteen thousand in dust when you had the chance?" Slocum asked, around a mouth full of horseshoe nails. He was stooped over, facing Pete's rear, the front hoof between his knees.

Montoya slapped a hand to his heart theatrically. "*Señor Capitán!* We are loyal!"

About as loyal as rabid skunks, Slocum was thinking, but he said, "To a Confederacy that's been squashed flat for better'n twenty years? That's some kind of loyalty."

Montoya gave him a curious look. "You were a hero in the first war."

Slocum pounded in another nail. "Whoever told you that was exaggerating. I just did what I was told. Went where they sent me and did it some more."

Montoya rubbed his mustache. "You killed many men, though?"

Slocum paused. What was this *bandido* getting at anyway? He said, "I suppose. Many soldiers." He tapped in the last nail and set it.

"Sometimes modesty is not such a good thing, I think," Montoya said, gazing off into the distance and scratching his backside thoughtfully. Then he looked at Slocum. "You will not try to charge for his service? You will not sell this stud, but yet you do not ask a fee?"

Slocum let the stud's hoof down and slowly stood erect, easing the kinks out of his back. Between Maddie last night and setting the shoe this afternoon, his back was a little touchy. A corporal walked by, stopped and stared, then hurried on his way. What was it with these boys? Didn't any of them talk?

He turned his attention to the bandit chief. "Nope. No charge. I'd like to see some spotted horses down here. Course, you won't get all color, breeding him to solid mares. But you'll get more than, say, sixty or seventy percent spotted stock, and they should all be fair-sized. Even-tempered too."

It was the truth. He didn't want any money. He didn't give a damn how many mares they let old Pete climb on top of, so long as he got him back in one piece and didn't have to kill somebody to get him.

The point of all this contention had dozed off. Slocum turned toward the horse's head, saying, "Wake up, you old buzzard," when he couldn't raise the leg. Pete blinked sleepily and allowed his hoof to be placed, right side up, on Slocum's thigh. Slocum went to work with the file.

Montoya nodded. "He is the polite horse. Never savages the mares. I myself once owned a sorrel stud that would kill as many mares as he settled. I had to cut him. It made me very sad, for the colts he got were fine indeed. Much fire and speed. Would you like to have your pistols and rifle back, *amigo*? Also your knife?"

This bandit was as full of twists and turns as the canyons he guarded. Slocum said, "I'm near naked without 'em." He let the appy's hoof down, patted the horse on the shoulder, and stood up. "Why? You got 'em?"

Montoya smiled wide, showing the eyetooth gap. "No. But I know who does, maybe."

Dinner was late, because of the wedding.

Slocum hadn't had a chance to get back to talk to Maddie again. She sent him a daggered look just before the only other woman he'd seen in the canyon, a stout Mexican woman who he assumed was Maria, the head cook, lowered Maddie's skimpy veil and handed her over to Daddy Jim.

The bridal gown she wore was a simple peasant blouse and skirt, the groom was under armed guard, the music was a mouth harp coming from the porch, and the "preacher" was General Turnbull, the man who had pummeled her in Chicago.

Still, Maddie was a beautiful bride. When Frank lifted her veil at the end, her face was shining, and the kiss she gave him was almost shy.

Slocum should have known better than to believe it, though. After the couple was toasted with champagne and the groom (once more under house arrest) was led meekly back to the barracks, Maddie gave him a discreet— but painful—kick to the shins.

"Why didn't you come?" she hissed, before saying in a louder voice, dripping with shy enthusiasm, "Why, thank you for your congratulations, Mr. Slocum. I'm just overjoyed! And I'll convey your felicitations to Frank."

He felt like kicking her back, but settled for stepping on her foot. "I tried to," he whispered. "Come to my room tonight." Then he said aloud, "I'm sure you'll be real happy, Mrs. Osborn. Allow me to offer my best wishes."

Then Daddy Jim swept her off toward a group of officers.

Carrying a champagne glass, Slocum wandered out front into the dusky light. Lingering on the wide front porch were a couple of enlisted men, one of whom was the mouth harp player. He launched into "Dixie" as Slocum sat down.

"Ain't you supposed to stand up for that one, Slocum?" said a voice to his right.

He stared into the shadows. The voice sounded familiar, but he couldn't see the face, just a man in profile, whittling. Squinting, Slocum said, "Who's that? Judging by today, I thought non-coms weren't allowed to talk to me."

"Oh, they's allowed," the man said. The voice was irritatingly familiar. "They's just afraid to. A man who slays dragons, chops out their livers, and eats 'em raw for breakfast ain't to be took lightly. Mex *bandidos* appear to be a little braver, though. Maybe they ain't got no livers to start with."

"What the—"

"Listen up, Slocum. These boys a'yourn are up to no good. I reckon by now you already kenned that. The rumor is that they've got a hundred men already in Tucson, waitin' for the word, and another hundred in Prescott."

"How—"

"Shut up. I know you already know about Tucson. If you hadn't spent half the night messin' with that woman—say, she's a yowler, ain't she?—I could'a told you the easy way, but no, old Slocum gets a hitch in his bumpers, and—"

"Yancy!" It had to be Yancy Tate. Nobody else would say a "hitch in his bumpers" when he meant an itch in his britches. Nobody else would hide outside his window for half the night, listening while he and Maddie made love, or call her a "yowler." Fast-talking, slick-as-a-whistle Yancy Tate, who just seemed to pop up every now and then, just when the going got dangerous. Usually when the danger involved the nation's safety. Slocum had been through more than one ripsnorter with him. And he usually came out on the short end of the stick, come to think of it.

"Keep your voice down," said Yancy.

Slocum drained his champagne glass and set it down with a *thump*. "I ought to knock you into next week, you crazy bastard," he growled.

"Now, Slocum." The voice took on a creamy

texture. "As I recall, Opal Ann was a real generous girl, and—"

"Not about Opal," Slocum groused. "About Silver City."

"Oh. Well, now, I didn't mean to leave you hangin' out to dry, Slocum, honest. Sometimes these things cain't be helped. You got out of it, though, and with all your parts intact, didn't you? Got out of it just fine, as I recall. Ouch!"

Slocum smiled. "Teach you to whittle in the dark, you dumb cracker."

Yancy sucked at his finger. "I might be a cracker, but at least I don't sleep with no ladies the night afore their weddin's to certain colonels who are more chock full'a nuts than Aunt Martha's pecan pie. Can you get out of here?"

The harmonica man finished "Dixie" and swung into "The Yellow Rose of Texas."

Slocum said, "Don't know the way. I can't even get my damn guns back. Furthermore, I can't figure out why the devil they haven't stood me up against a wall and shot me. And what are you doing here?"

"Business, Slocum. Just business. Now listen up. General Miles is—"

The front door banged open. It was O'Hara, the rosy bloom of a champagne smile on his face. "Here you are, Captain! Dinner's on the table, and quite an extravaganza it is!" He dug into his pocket, then tossed a coin to the mouth harp player. "Thank you, thank you.

You boys get on down to the barracks now. General Turnbull has ordered two glasses of beer for every man, by way of celebration."

Slocum stood up and followed O'Hara into the hacienda. Yancy Tate had disappeared into the gloom.

14

Dinner, aside from the still-flowing champagne and the occasional toast, was uneventful.

Maddie, the groomless bride, sat at the foot of the table, nibbling on tortillas and paté— and some repulsive concoction that Slocum learned was pickled squid—and looking sweetly pliant. General Turnbull stared at her when he thought no one was looking, and Slocum figured it was only a matter of time before he hooked her up with Chicago. Slocum didn't know exactly what that would mean, but he would have taken odds that it wasn't going to be pleasant.

Daddy Jim O'Hara, alias Jimmy Ray Osborn, alias the Butcher of Bent Horn, was animated. He had a private bottle of champagne to go along with the grits, bloody roast beef, frijoles, and artichoke hearts he shoveled down, asking for a fresh bottle halfway through the meal.

For his part, Slocum pushed his food around on his plate, pretending gaiety while he stewed over what little information Yancy had been able to give him before they were interrupted.

A hundred men in Tucson and another hundred in Prescott? Counting the men in camp, that gave O'Hara and Turnbull over 450 soldiers. And Yancy had mentioned General Miles, the commandant in Tucson: the man who had captured Geronimo and sent him packing to some swamp in Florida.

What did Yancy want Slocum to do? Break out and ride to warn Miles? Warn him against what, though? That a ragtag little outfit with delusions of grandeur was about to set siege to the Presidio?

Miles would laugh him out of his office, if he didn't throw him in the stockade.

Provided he could get to his office. Provided he could find his way out of these canyons and past the *bandidos*.

Yancy was crazy as a loon.

Throughout dinner, Carlos Montoya was oddly silent. That was, until dessert arrived—Mexican wedding cookies surrounding a small, white cake. Then he rose, quite solemnly, and made a grand, slurry toast, which included the bride and absent groom, along with such diverse elements as James O'Hara, Geronimo, General Turnbull, old Pete, the Confederate States of America (Reformed), and Cortez.

When there was a palpable silence at the end—probably from the drunken guests not knowing whether he was finished—he thrust his glass up in the air forcefully with a *"Salud!"* There was an audible sigh of relief as Montoya slouched into his chair again and closed his eyes. Everyone drank.

Everyone except Maddie, Slocum noticed. He'd switched to coffee, and he could tell that her glass was filled with water. Smart girl. They were sitting smack dab in the eye of a twister, and the last thing they needed was to settle back and let the breeze take them.

Dinner ended in much the same manner as it had the night before. O'Hara rose and excused Maddie, who went silently to her room, and then the table was cleared and the brandy and cigars brought out.

The Mexican boy slipped out the door with a piece of cake, Slocum noticed. Probably to take it to the bridegroom. He'd be damned if he wasn't feeling a little sorry for Frank.

Not much, but a little.

O'Hara cleared his throat until the table was silent, except for the soft snores of Montoya, who seemed to have passed out next to Slocum. O'Hara, his eyes slightly unfocused with drink, said, "Well, Captain Slocum. You've seen our little operation. Are you with us?"

Slocum had expected a little more preamble. He said, "Well, now, Jim, I think you've got a fine idea here." He paused to take a puff on his cigar. "But to be honest, I don't hardly know what you're up to. Seems to me you ain't got a tenth enough soldiers to start the war again. Not that I don't think it's a good idea, mind. I just can't fathom how you're going to do it."

General Turnbull sat up straight. Well, as straight as he could, considering all the champagne—and now brandy—he'd taken in. If Slocum was any judge, Turnbull would be up half the night puking.

"*Suh!*" he announced, his Southern accent more pronounced with drink. "Ah believe our esteemed associate has asked you a direct question."

Slocum regarded him with one brow cocked. "And I'd be happy to answer, General, if I thought this outfit had a purpose besides marchin' up and down in the middle of nowhere."

Turnbull started to struggle to his feet, but O'Hara motioned him down. "You're a wise man, Captain," he said, and something about the way he said it led Slocum to believe that he wasn't as drunk as he was putting on. "Of course, you'd like to know a little more about our aims."

"Cleanse the race!" said a very blond, very drunken lieutenant catty-corner from Slocum. Petersen, if Slocum remembered correctly.

Another lieutenant, next to the first, said, "That's right. No niggers, Injuns, Gypsies, or Jews. No Greeks or Eye-talians neither. No Mex—"

"Cosgrove!" barked General Turnbull. "That will be enough. Take yourself to quarters."

But Slocum knew that Montoya, despite his snores, had heard. Just a little twitch at the corner of his mustache gave him away.

As the lieutenant scraped back his chair, the *bandido* pretended to rouse at the sound, to come out of a stupor. "Is the dinner over?" he asked, blinking.

Slocum stood up. "Jim, if y'all don't mind, maybe we can continue this in the morning? I don't know about you, but I'm ready for some sleep. Like you said, mornin' comes early around here."

O'Hara concurred. "So it does, my boy. Gentlemen, you'll excuse me too?" He pushed back from the table, rose with some effort, and preceded Slocum down the hall. At the first room, he stopped, hand on the latch, and turned.

"Think about it, Captain," he said, and if Slocum hadn't seen him put away two bottles of champagne with his own eyes, he never would have known, by the man's demeanor, that he'd touched a drop. "I suggest you think about it long and hard. But not too long."

Slocum was still thinking about it an hour later as he paced his room in the dark, smoking the last of his dinner cigar and waiting for Yancy, waiting for Maddie.

Yancy being there had complicated things, that was for sure.

Obviously, the boys in Washington figured Jim O'Hara to be more than an eccentric windbag with money to burn. They expected trouble, or else they wouldn't have sent Yancy. Slocum was sure the harmonica player was in it too, for Yancy had talked freely in front of him.

And there was Montoya. Something was going on under the big Mexican's surface. Would any self-respecting Mexican listen to what that peckerwood shavetail had said and not react to it? No, he was up to something.

Slocum wondered if the Mexican government could have a finger in stopping this too, then wondered why. Why help stop a revolution in a neighboring country, particularly one you weren't on the friendliest terms with? Texas, New Mexico, Arizona—it was one long war with Mexico, just years between the battles.

But regardless, even though he didn't know the message, it looked like he was stuck with courier duty, if and when he could shake himself free.

General Miles was going to laugh his ass off.

If Slocum made it that far.

There was a knock at the door. Slocum lit the lamp and said, "Come in," sure it was Maddie.

It was Jim O'Hara, dressed in that green silk

robe Maddie had been wearing the night before. It had looked a great deal better pooled and puddled on her than it did stretched over his frame. He stood in open doorway, filling it completely. "You're still up, Captain." He ran a hand over his shiny scalp, then lit a cigar. "Couldn't sleep after all?"

"Guess not," said Slocum.

"Well, I wouldn't wait up any longer. Not for Maddie."

Slocum stiffened. "Maddie?"

"No. There won't be a repeat of last night's performance," O'Hara said, shaking out his match and dropping it to the tiles. "Oh, don't look so surprised. I know a great deal about what goes on around here, Captain."

Slocum spoke slowly, measuring his words. "And still, you let her marry Frank. Your son."

O'Hara shrugged. A flake of ash fell from his cigar, floated to the floor. "Once a whore, always a whore. She was entitled to one last fling. I decided to let her take it."

Slocum pushed back his anger. This wasn't the time or the place. "I doubt that marriage was legal."

"Oh, it was legal enough. Turnbull's a justice of the peace back home in . . . Well, back where he comes from. We don't talk much about the past here. Besides, it's consummated now."

Slocum raised a brow. "You let Frank out?"

O'Hara chuckled. "No, he's still under house arrest. I consummated it. Power of attorney, you know. I am Frank, Frank is me."

Slocum couldn't speak, couldn't even move for fear he'd throttle the man. He heard himself whisper, "You raped her."

"Not rape, exactly. More like fulfilling a legal obligation. I must say, I hardly expected her to fight me the way she did. She's been such a pliant little wench these past two years. Gave me some song and dance about Frank planning the first holdup."

He shook his head, smiling. "Just playing for time, of course. Frank isn't that smart. Didn't know she had it in her to make up a tale like that, let alone claw me. Practically made mincemeat of my back. I must say, I rather enjoyed it. So did she, after a time."

Slocum felt his breath coming in short, sharp bursts, his hands curling into fists. To attack this man would write his own death warrant, but he was beginning not to care.

O'Hara puffed on his cigar thoughtfully, oblivious to—or perhaps enjoying—Slocum's dilemma, and scratched his belly through green silk. "Well, enough of that. Don't try to see her tonight. Her room is locked, and I've taken the liberty of posting guards outside her window, and yours."

Stepping out into the hall with surprising nimbleness, he closed the door with a "Sleep tight, Captain." Slocum heard a key turn in the lock.

Too late, Slocum threw himself at the door, and nearly had the latch yanked off it when a voice from behind him whispered, "Whoa up there, John. Hold your horses."

He wheeled around. "Yancy, you sonofabitch! Why didn't you tell me—"

Yancy Tate, on the outside of the window, held up a hand. "Didn't know, old son. But you ain't gonna help that gal none by rippin' the house down. Leave her be to her own misery."

Slocum crossed the room in two strides and thrust his arm and shoulder through the open window, grabbing Yancy by the throat. "Get me out of here," he hissed. "Tell me where to find my goddamn guns and I'll get myself out."

When he realized Yancy couldn't talk, he let go, and Yancy doubled over and gulped for air, losing his cap in the process.

"Judas priest, Slocum," he wheezed after a minute, picking up his cap and dusting it on his leg. "It ain't my fault. Told you the sonofabitch was nuttier than a pecan pie, didn't I? Here I am, tryin' to help your ornery ass, and you near to strangle me!"

"If you're gonna help me, then do it and quit gabbin'," Slocum growled. As far as he was concerned, when Jim O'Hara had forced himself on Maddie, he'd burst the last thin skin of sanity cloaking this place. Slocum just wanted to put as much distance as possible between it and him, and take Maddie with him. Maybe kill O'Hara on his way out.

But Yancy said, "Sorry, *compadre,* can't do 'er." He settled the cap on his head. "Hard enough for me to worm my way into sentry duty."

When Slocum stared at him, Yancy explained. "I traded with a fella who traded with a fella who traded with a fella. Fella I traded with sort of busted his leg, real sudden-like. You gonna let me talk now?"

Slocum exhaled slowly. "All right," he said. "Talk."

Yancy began. "These boys've been out here, growin' like a goddamn tumor, for 'bout four years. Get all their financin' from O'Hara's gold mine."

"Why don't you just close him down?" Slocum said.

Yancy grimaced. "Wanted to. Bunch of Washington assholes said to wait and see, even when it turned out he didn't exactly own the land he was minin'. And then they said it was too late, we'd better catch 'em in the act. So that's what we're doin'. Always got to do everythin' the hard way. I swan, those peckerwoods couldn't produce a keg of beer but what they'd pay sixty dollars to make it and kill three people in the process."

"Yancy?"

"Sorry." Yancy smiled. "I just get goin' sometimes, don't I? Anyway, Miles knows what's cookin' out here. A few of his officers too, but that's it. O'Hara's got infiltrators. Mostly civilians, but some military. Don't know how many."

"Why doesn't Miles just storm the place?"

"Casualties'd be too high. They's only two entrances to this canyon, the one you came in and the south one. O'Hara'd just put his men up there and they'd have them a turkey shoot."

"Then cut off their supplies."

Yancy shook his head. "They'd just get 'em from the Mexican side of the Crows. Most of the stuff comes up from there now anyways."

"This whole thing is crazy," Slocum said in exasperation. "They can't think they could take the South back!"

"They don't want the South," Yancy said, his face gone serious. "They're only after the Arizona Territory. For starters anyway." He gestured toward the dark barracks. "Most of them boys out yonder think they're fightin' for the lost glory of the South and the tarnished honor of Jeff Davis, and maybe so they can own their own slaves to beat on. But what they're really gonna die for is O'Hara's little utopia. An all-white state. There's this feller up to Massachusetts who wrote a book on it ten, fifteen years back, bunch'a hogwash about the purity of the races, how folks have got to breed true."

Slocum stared at him.

Yancy sighed. "Oh, he wasn't broad about it at all. No, sir. White stickin' to white, and he was real picky about what kinds of white. Ruled out the Russians and the Czechs and the Spanish right off the bat, same thing for the Jews and the Arabs and the Persians. Got his doubts about the French, and don't trust the Italians. I hear they laughed him out of the state. But O'Hara took him dead serious, and that's what he's aimin' for. You notice how all the officers have English or Irish or Scotch names? One Scandinavian feller."

Slocum nodded. "That asshole Petersen."

Yancy nodded. "Well, that's all the kinds O'Hara's gonna let into his little dreamland. And only the Irish who'll convert. Can't have any Papists, no, sir. Some northern European too, I guess—maybe Dutch, maybe German— if their pedigrees check out, but no colored folks, no Mexicans or Indians, no—"

Slocum broke in. "What the hell's he plan to do with the ones that are already here?"

Yancy stared at him levelly. "Guess."

Slocum's stomach turned over. He'd never given it a thought before. He tried to picture the Territory without Melvin Brothers' Lumber, or without Sophie Silverberg's chophouse in Prescott, or without Tony Napoli's hand-tooled tack.

He thought, all in a rush, of Maria Seven Fingers and Joaquin Gonzales and Tracker Bob Washington and Xavier Saperstein and countless others. People he'd shared meals with, laughed with, shared hard times with, people he owed his life to. And then he pictured them dead, heaped up, burned out, shot, hanged.

Murdered.

He looked at Yancy, his face hard and set. "What do you want me to do?"

Yancy nodded, as if he understood the pictures that had just played through Slocum's mind. "Just go along with him for right now. Do whatever O'Hara wants. He's waitin' on a message from one of his fellers in Tucson. He's been waitin' on it for nigh on two years now, so you're most likely off the hook. All you've got to do is hold on until he leaves, which is Saturday. If the message don't come by then, you can take the lady and we'll get you out."

"And if it does come?"

Yancy shouldered his gun again. "Then you get on that fancy horse of yours and ride to Tucson like the devil hisself was after you. Montoya'll show you the way. Don't stop for Maddie."

"Don't stop for Maddie?"

"Don't stop for nothin'. And don't talk to nobody but Miles, you got that? Nobody but Miles. Tell him it's started."

"Why can't you do it?"

"Because, old son, I'll likely be dead."

15

The next morning, Slocum emerged at six-thirty, once again too late for breakfast. He found Jim O'Hara in his usual place, rocking on the front porch and smoking a cigar. It was still cool, and he hadn't broken a sweat yet.

He looked up when Slocum came out, and without preamble called, "Pablito! Breakfast for Captain Slocum!"

He swept a massive arm toward the chair beside his wide rocker. "Sit, Captain, sit. No standing on ceremonies around here." He laughed as Slocum sat down. "Well, I suppose there's some ceremony," he said over the sounds of drilling troops. "Yes indeed. Quite a bit, as a matter of fact. Tell me, Captain Slocum, have you given thought to our little conversation last night?"

Slocum leaned back. Be agreeable, Yancy had said. Well, he could be as agreeable as the next man. Maybe more. He smiled. "Which one, Jim? The one about joining up, or the one about hands off the lady?"

"Touché!" said O'Hara, piercing the air with a wave of his Havana. "The former, of course.

Needless to say, there needn't be any further discussion about the latter. With anyone. Especially Maddie."

"Point taken, Jim. Now, about this signing-up business. I'm all for cleaning the trash out of this Territory, getting rid of the Indians and the Mexicans and the like."

That pleased the fat bastard. O'Hara nodded and smiled.

"But I reckon I'll need to know just what I'm getting into." Slocum stretched his arms wide, over the back of the chair, and tilted his head toward O'Hara. "Frankly, Jim, I think you boys have got a snowball's chance in hell of startin' the war up again. You've only got around two hundred men. Now, I can see that you've whipped 'em into fighting shape, but two hundred's a drop in the bucket. If a man could set his sights lower—say, just take Arizona, maybe southern California in time—and if he had a couple hundred more men, and if he could manage to somehow take, say, Tucson for starters. Maybe Prescott. The capital's in Prescott this week, but Tucson's got General Miles, and if you could wipe him out . . ."

Slocum shook his head. "Nope. It's too much. You've only got half enough men to take part of Arizona, Jim. I don't see how in hell you can pull off bringing the whole South into it. I'm afraid I'll have to decline."

O'Hara was silent, for just then the boy brought out the breakfast tray. Slocum saw he'd done better this morning—there was a thick slice of ham besides the bread and jam and coffee (and fortunately, no pickled squid)—but O'Hara's reticence bothered him. Maybe he'd gone too far.

Slocum leaned forward, slapped the ham between two pieces of bread, and took a bite. Might as well go out well fed.

But O'Hara was only waiting for the boy's footsteps to recede back into the kitchen. He rocked forward and leaned toward Slocum, his elbows resting on his pudgy knees.

"You're an astute man, Captain. Contrary to what the men have been told—all except the officers, of course—we have no plans to repeat the folly of Jefferson Davis. No indeed, sir."

His voice lowered to a whisper. "As we speak, I have an additional four hundred men—one hundred and fifty in Tucson, one hundred in Prescott, and fifty each in Phoenix, Flagstaff, and Bisbee. One word from me, and they will effectively cripple all communication with the outside world, put those localities under martial law, and immediately fan out to subjugate the lesser communities. Put the torch to the Mormon settlements. Clean out the reservations. Wipe these stinking Mexicans off the face of the earth."

He leaned back again. "I had thought at one time they'd make a good slave population, but I've since reconsidered. There is an intrinsic cleverness to the race that doesn't fit it for slavery. Besides, our proximity to the Mexican border does not bode well for such a venture. Now, there are the niggers, of course, but popular opinion in the States being what it is . . ."

He stopped to re-light his cigar. Slocum waited. He didn't have to wait long.

"The Mormons are mostly white people," O'Hara continued, puffing. "Well, they're all white, but I mean the right kind of white—and I believe they're onto something with this polygamy thing. But they owe allegiance to that bastard Brigham Young up in Utah. I will not have that." He paused a moment, frowning. "You're not Catholic, are you?"

Slocum swallowed the bite of sandwich in his mouth. "Not that I know of."

"Good, good. Where was I? Oh. Slaves. No, I think we can do just fine if we operate on our own merits. No, there'll be no slaves in our little Eden."

"Smart," Slocum said. "You don't plan to take the whole South then?"

"Just Arizona. Later on, we'll worry about California and New Mexico. When the people see what a utopian climate we've created . . ." O'Hara gazed off into the distance, a dreamy smile on his round face.

"Imagine it, Captain. Arizona, turned into the garden of Eden, and renamed New Albion. A pure white race, living in peace and harmony in a land named after the dwelling place of the most ancient of pure races. I have plans to divert the Colorado River. We'll dam the Salt and the Gila. We'll make this state—this country!—into an oasis, a model of white efficiency. Think of it! Orchards on the desert! There'll be no need for white hoods and burning crosses here, no, sir. Not after you finish your job."

Slocum didn't think he was going to like the answer, but he asked, "My job?"

"Why, to stamp out the seeds of pollution, of course! Your most excellent reputation precedes you, my dear captain. A crack sniper. A good man in close combat. Good? The best! I've heard all about your exploits at the Battle of Hasty Rise and how you went through the enemy like a scythe at Kimchucket. You're just the man—both in courage and in temperament—to do the job."

Slocum had never been at either of those places, in fact had only heard of one of them: Kimchucket. It was called a battle, but in truth Quantrill's men, in unison with Bloody Bill Anderson, had set upon a Kansas camp, a safe-stop for runaway slaves. They had slaughtered 134 men, women, and children, all unarmed. He'd heard that the men had fought back with sticks, but sticks couldn't stand up to bayonets and bullets.

Slocum had been wounded and was out of it by then, thank God, but somebody thought he'd been there. Went through the enemy like a scythe? Jesus. The rumor mill had been working double time. He made himself say, "You flatter me, Jim."

O'Hara waved a pudgy hand, the cigar leaving a smoke trail in the still air. "I don't believe in flattery, Captain. I believe in deeds. After the initial proceedings, you'll be given a company of men. I want you to rid New Albion—Arizona—of all its trash. I don't care how you do it. Just clean out the vermin."

If Slocum had his way, he would have ridded the Territory of one big, fat rat right then and there. But Yancy's words still rang in his ear.

He said, "Fine by me. But what do I get out of it? Other that the pleasure of the job, that is."

O'Hara smiled. "I like a man who enjoys his work. You'll be given ten thousand acres, Captain, the same as all the other officers. Ten thousand acres in the garden spot of the Western Hemisphere, to do whatever you like with. Raise cattle, raise horses, raise Cain."

"And in the meantime?"

"Sixty dollars a month, in gold. All pay is held by me, of course, until after the revolution. No need for money here."

Slocum figured if the other officers had been in it for four years, they had a good chunk of money coming. If they ever saw it.

"All right," he said. "I'm in. But I'm not

wearing a uniform, seeing as how I'm Special Duty."

"Done," said O'Hara.

"And I want my guns back. Danged if I don't feel naked without 'em."

"Done as well." O'Hara pointed to the gun box at the other end of the porch. "Your arms have been waiting for you since last night, Captain."

As Slocum walked over and proceeded to buckle his Colts back on, O'Hara said, "Captain, you understand that none of what I've just told you is to be discussed. With anyone."

Slocum slid his knife back in his boot. "All right."

He had just cracked open the Winchester when Maddie walked out on the porch. She saw him, but walked straight to O'Hara and gave him a peck on the cheek. "And how's my Daddy Jim this morning?" she asked brightly.

Slocum had been having visions of her lying on the floor, crying and bruised and bloody, after last night. But this?

O'Hara said, "Just fine, my little sugar plum. Just dandy. Captain Slocum here has consented to ride with us, Maddie."

"That's nice," she said, and began to rub O'Hara's shoulders. "Did I miss breakfast again?"

Disgusted with O'Hara and Maddie and the world in general, Slocum stepped down off the porch.

"Find Lieutenant Petersen," O'Hara called after him. "He'll show you around."

He had his tour of the place before noon. A too-respectful Lieutenant Petersen showed him the barracks, the granary, and the armory buildings. As Petersen pointed out one feature after another, Slocum realized how well prepared O'Hara was for war. Cook wagons, troop wagons, rolling cannons, Gatling guns: You name it, he had it.

Petersen told him that besides the stock in the corral, more horses were grazing in the next canyon over, to the south. Four hundred, all told. Besides the horses, there was a small beef herd, also in another canyon, and hogs and chickens at the far end of this one.

He nodded curtly at each new description the lieutenant offered. Petersen was one tight-assed little bastard. Not one wrinkle in that uniform, not one wrong step, not one wrong word. Annoyingly polite.

Slocum had seen men like that before, in the army. They usually got killed right off once the fighting started. They stood up because the rule book didn't say to duck, waited for an order to fire when the enemy was ten feet away and leaping with bayonet. Some such nonsense.

Men like Petersen died quick, but they died by the rules. As if that was any comfort.

They were just walking up toward the hacienda again, up a wide and dusty palo-verde-canopied lane between the corrals and the rear barracks, when Petersen checked his timepiece and took his leave. "You'll excuse me, sir," he said, as stiffly formal as he'd been for the entire tour. "I have an appointment with General Turnbull."

He saluted. Slocum returned it lackadaisically, then watched as Petersen marched toward Turnbull's office, looking for all the world like he had a great big cob up his backside.

"That one, he is a piece of work, *no*?"

Grinning, Slocum turned to see Montoya walking up from the corrals to meet him. "That he most certainly is," Slocum agreed.

"I see you have found your guns. The rifle too."

Slocum nodded, and stuck the Winchester under his arm, barrel pointed toward the ground. He'd been carrying it all morning. "They turned up, just like magic."

"You are lucky they are the guns you started with, *Capitán*. I had to convince one *hombre* to let that rifle go. Well, the Colts too, but especially that Winchester. It is a very fine piece." He scratched his belly. "So you told the fat one you will ride for him?"

Slocum pulled out his fixings and began to roll up a quirlie. "Let's say I was agreeable."

"The lieutenant showed you everything?"

Slocum gave a lick to the cigarette, and stuck it in his mouth. "Near about everything. One major oversight, though."

Montoya smiled, the droopy ends of his mustache twitching. "I could show you this. Come, look at the horses."

Slocum flicked a lucifer into life as he followed Montoya toward the corrals, lighting his smoke with cupped hands. They came to Pete's corral first, where a couple of troopers leaned over the fence.

"You see, *Señor Capitán*?" Montoya said in a loud voice. "This morning he rests from the ladies."

The troopers scrambled to attention and gave a salute. One looked scared to death, the other one cocky but nervous. Slocum returned the salute and said, "As you were," but both men hurriedly left the area.

Pete moseyed over to the fence line, and Slocum scratched him between the eyes. "What's with those boys?" he asked. "Yesterday nobody'd look at me, they were so busy runnin' away, and today they're salutin' their britches off."

The Mexican grinned. "There were others?"

"All through Petersen's tour." The appaloosa lowered his head so that Slocum could scratch his ears.

"Ah, but you see, they know you have been accepted. They know you are to ride with us.

Also, they are afraid you will eat them for breakfast."

"What?"

"Didn't you know, *Capitán*?" Montoya asked, his face unreadable. "You stab babies on the bayonet, one, two, three. You cut the hair from the living man, then make him watch while you have his woman. You jerk the flesh of virgins on thistle bushes, and chew it while you ride into battle."

Montoya smiled suddenly, his voice scolding. "Señor, have you no mercy?"

Slocum choked on the smoke from his quirlie. "Reckon not," he said between coughs.

Montoya slapped him on the back, laughing softly. "Come with me, killer of women and children."

They walked down the line of corrals, Montoya pointing out one horse or another (mostly for the benefit of stray troopers), until they had walked nearly to the end of the row. A *bandido* with a blackened eye took one look at them and left, walking briskly up the far side of the corrals.

"He think I'm a baby-eater too?"

The Mexican shook his head. "That is Manuel. He is the one who liked your rifle too much. You see that, *Capitán*?" Montoya pointed past the milling horses to a small building standing alone and nearly cloaked by the palo verde growing thick about it, a building guarded by many more troops than its size would warrant. The windows were barred, where Slocum could see windows through the trees, and there was a huge padlock on the door. Montoya pushed back his sombrero to show the line of lighter skin the sun seldom touched, and smiled broadly. "The gates of Heaven."

Slocum ground out the quirlie beneath his boot. "The gold."

"They don't go in often," Montoya said, starting back toward Pete's corral. "Only when supplies are to be paid for, or when the whores come."

"The whores?"

"They bring them from Mexico every six months. Conchita Romero's girls, two wagons of them. They stay a week, they go home rich. Some of these men have been here for four years, *Capitán*. They do not mind if they get an ugly one."

"Montoya?"

"What?" Montoya hiked a brow and smirked. "You do not mind an ugly one either?"

"No, I mean, yes. I mean, do you know what's really going on around here? What O'Hara's up to?"

Montoya's face went from mildly amused to deadly serious. "Oh, we know. We wait, that is all. We wait until he rides. Maybe tomorrow, maybe next year. But when he rides, we take the gold. Maybe we take a few pieces of O'Hara too."

"Save some for me," Slocum said.

"The gold, or O'Hara?"

"Both, I reckon."

16

Maddie paced her room, up and down, looking out the window each time she passed it, which was every four steps. Step, step, turn. Step, step, look. Step, step, turn.

What was wrong with him? Hadn't he talked to that Mexican bandit long enough? She tried to will him to glance her way.

Come to me, Slocum, she thought. *Come to Maddie. Come to Mama.*

It didn't work.

He'd already wandered down the lane and out of sight, and she thought he was never coming back, but now he *was* back and she couldn't get his attention.

Step, step, look.

Nothing. His back was toward her. She could signal to that Mexican he was with, but he'd probably run and tell Daddy Jim the first chance he got.

She didn't know what had gotten into Daddy Jim. Well, other than that he was a liar and a cheat, that he'd made her marry a loony, that he was getting ready to start a war, and that he'd forbade her to have further contact with Slocum.

Come to think of it, what *hadn't* gotten into Daddy Jim?

She came to the window again just as Slocum turned her way. She signaled frantically, afraid to make a sound, and—thank God—he saw her. He didn't give much sign, just a little tip of his head, but she relaxed.

He parted company with the *bandido* and slowly began to mosey toward her, stopping to roll a cigarette.

She cursed when a trio of soldiers coming up the wide, dusty path nearly ran into him, and stopped to salute. Slocum lit his smoke and shook out the match before he got around to returning it, and the three men moved on quickly.

She heard one of them say, "Aw, he ain't so tough," before one of the others hushed him and led him away by his arm.

Slocum came within ten feet of her window and stopped, smoking. His profile was toward her, and distorted by the palo verdes, which grew thick on this side of the hacienda.

"Why didn't you come earlier?" she said in a low voice. "I've been going crazy!"

He flicked a glance toward her, and she added, "Maybe that's a bad choice of words. But where have you been?"

He took a drag on his cigarette. The smoke rose up through pale green needles. "Heard you were busy. That was quite a little show you put on this morning with your daddy."

Show? What show?

"What does that have to do with anything? It was just normal, that's all. I've got to keep up appearances, especially with him."

Slocum took another draw on the cigarette. Before, she'd liked it that the trees were here. Now she wished that they were gone. It was like talking to him through a pale green haze. She couldn't see his face, and she wanted to. She needed to see it.

He said, "I'm sorry he came to you last night, Maddie. I didn't know about it until it was too late. But you don't have to act like everything is so goddamned normal!"

The man was exasperating! She said, "Slocum, honestly, I don't have the least notion of what you're blathering about. Nobody came to me last night. Just Daddy Jim, telling me he'd posted guards. Granted, I suppose that's not normal, posting guards, I mean, but—"

Suddenly Slocum turned toward her. "He didn't touch you?"

She rolled her eyes. "Of course not. He couldn't. He never could. What I'm trying to tell you, Slocum, is that Frank—"

"What do you mean he never could?"

"Christ! Because he got his . . ." There just wasn't a delicate way to say this.

"What do you mean, Maddie?"

She sighed and rolled her eyes. Just blurt it

out, that was the way. "Because they shot his balls off in the war, that's why. Half his pecker too. *Now* can I tell you about Frank?"

Slocum had the usual male reaction. He bent over, cringing, and grabbed at his crotch. He was probably thinking what a big target he had.

"Stop smirking," he grumbled at last.

"Sorry. Now can I tell you about Frank?"

"Yeah, yeah, tell me all about good old Frank." He was standing up straight again and had turned away, distracted by something up the path.

"Frank said that I never had the consumption. Daddy Jim made it up to get me out of Chicago."

"A friend to mankind, that's Jim O'Hara," Slocum declared. He took a step away to see something better. Something that was up at the front of the hacienda, something that for her was blocked by the trees.

She ignored him. "But you'll never believe *why* he wanted to get me away. Why he had me take his name. See, the land that he's mining—"

"Captain Slocum!" someone called from up the way, up toward the front of the hacienda.

Before she knew what was happening, Slocum had crossed the distance between them, leaned through the window and kissed her— kissed her quite forcefully, in fact.

He growled, "I'll be back for you, Maddie,"

into her ear, and then he was gone.

He left her shaking in her shoes, and staring at a cigarette butt that smoldered beneath the palo verdes.

She sank down on her bed. Be back for her? He hadn't even said where he was going.

"Men," she said in disgust, and flopped back on the pillow.

When Slocum reached the front of the hacienda, a small crowd had gathered around the lathered horse tied to a porch rail and its dusty, civilian-clothed rider, who stood at attention beside O'Hara.

"Excellent, excellent," O'Hara was saying to General Turnbull. "We'll muster the men before dawn, have the last of them out of the canyons by nine, and bivouac on the western rim of the Santa Ritas by seven in the evening. General, you may start the wheels in motion."

Turnbull marched past Slocum, his subordinates buzzing around him like bees. In the middle of the plaza he gathered his men and began issuing orders. One or two at a time, the officers snapped a salute, then ran toward the corrals or the barracks or the wagons, barking orders.

O'Hara turned his attention to the rider. "Well done, MacNamara!" He waved a paper, the paper he'd held crumpled in his hand when Slocum first came up. "Well done, my boy! Maria! Pablito! Get this man something to eat!"

Slocum walked over to the horse and scraped lather off its neck with the flat of his hand. Montoya was behind him, and said softly, "I think it starts now. Don't worry about this horse, *Capitán*. We find someone to walk it out."

"Captain!" O'Hara was waving the paper at him.

Beyond the courtyard, a wagon, loaded with gear, rolled past. "There's sure a lot of ruckus around here this morning, Jim," Slocum observed.

"Indeed there is!" the fat man said enthusiastically. He was still sitting in his rocker, but his face was red, and sweat poured off his bald head and down his neck.

Maybe he'll just have a heart stroke and save everybody a lot of trouble, Slocum thought.

But O'Hara motioned him up on the porch, making little hurry-up waves with his hand. "Get something to eat," he said, "and then I want you to ride to the nearest town—that would be Oro Tiempo, I believe—and send some telegrams. I'll compose them while you're eating. Now go. Montoya, get his horse ready. Your men's too."

Slocum walked inside, where Maria was hurriedly slapping sandwiches together. If O'Hara thought he was going to send those telegrams, he was in for a big surprise. He'd ride straight to Tucson and bring General Nelson Miles up to date, and if Miles didn't throw him in the stockade for the rest of his natural life, he'd ride back in here and get Maddie.

And his fifteen hundred.

Maybe a lot more.

How much was ten percent of all the gold in their little iron-barred bank? Everything was working out better than expected.

He was only halfway through his sandwich when O'Hara shouted, "Captain Slocum!" again. For a fat man with no balls, O'Hara sure had a bellow.

Slocum threw the remains of his meal on the table, wiped his mouth on his sleeve, and went out. Now six wagons, covered with tarps, were lined up at the entrance to the canyon, with a seventh rolling into line. Montoya and his men were out front on their horses, and Montoya held the reins of Slocum's appaloosa.

O'Hara was waiting with a small sheaf of papers, folded in half, and a single gold eagle. "Guard these with your life, son," he said, handing the papers to Slocum. "Come back safe."

"And where am I supposed to report? After I send the wires, that is?"

"Why, right here! I'll be waiting. And when you come back, you can call me Mr. President!"

Slocum stood tall and snapped the crazy

bastard a salute, which he returned with a lop-sided smile. "Get going," O'Hara said.

Slocum slipped the papers into his saddle-bags and the coin into his pocket, then swung up on old Pete, who seemed none the worse for having had a harem.

Montoya said, "We show you the way, *Capitán*," and set his heels to his mount.

Slocum followed, congratulating himself on his good fortune.

Out past the waiting wagons they rode, then up again, over that twisting, treacherous serpentine trail along the cliff. He couldn't say it was much better sitting on the horse than flopped across it like a sack of potatoes. No one spoke, and it was just as well. It took all the concentration he and Pete had to keep from sliding off the edge.

Down, through a narrow passage tangled thick with *manzanita*, most of it dead, and finally out into a wide, scrubby canyon. As they started across it, Slocum said, "I thought they weren't going out until morning. Why's he stackin' those wagons now?"

"The wagons he takes tonight, through the eastern path. It is much better than this one, a real trail, but still too narrow for troops and wagons both."

"I thought you said there were only two ways in," Slocum said.

Montoya rolled his eyes. "I said there were

only two entrances to the big canyon, *Capitán*. There are many paths, though."

"Oh," said Slocum, feeling stupid.

"The wagons will go as far as the last canyon," Montoya continued, "and in the morning they will go out. The wagons are slow, so they have a head start, and will clear the path for the troops. This way, he hopes they will all meet up at the Santa Ritas at the same time. *Capitán* Slocum, did you read those messages you put in your saddlebags?"

Slocum reined in and twisted in his saddle to unbuckle the bag one-handed. He pulled out the papers and opened them.

Blank. All blank. That sonofabitch.

A gun cocked, followed by several more.

"Montoya?" Six *bandidos*, all with guns. All pointed at him.

"Ah, so sorry, señor. This is where we are to kill you and leave your body for the crows to pick. That is how Los Cuervos got the name, you know. The crows, picking the bones clean. Black crows, white bones. It is beautiful when you stop and think about it, *no*?"

"No," said Slocum. They had him ringed in. He didn't have a prayer.

The man next to Montoya, the man with the black eye, whispered something to Montoya in Spanish. In a long-suffering tone, Montoya said, *"Sí, Manuel, sí."* Then to Slocum: "You will toss Manuel the rifle, *por favor*?"

Slocum stared at him.

"Please, señor. It might get scratched by the bullet."

Slocum eased it out of the scabbard slowly.

Not a chance in hell. They'd mow him down before he could get a shot off. He thought about Maddie, alone in that camp with those madmen. He thought about Consuelo, in the room with the thousand broken mirrors at the Great Western's house in Yuma.

He thought about the good horses he'd ridden and the women he'd had, the men who'd been his friends and those who'd been his enemies.

"*Señor Capitán?*" Montoya was waiting.

He tossed the Winchester to Manuel, who caught it, grinning, and let out an echoing cry.

Montoya breathed, "Idiot."

"I'm sorry to see you go back on me, Montoya," Slocum said.

The bandit chief shrugged.

"Mind if I ask why?"

"The *patrón*'s orders. It seems you were not at a place called . . . something. Kercheckle? Kenchuckle?"

"Kimchucket," Slocum said, and swore under his breath. One slip. One lousy little slip.

"*Sí*, Kimchucket. O'Hara was there, but you were not. Also another battle called Hasty . . . Hasty Something."

"Hasty Rise."

"*Sí*. Hasty Rise. There was no such place. You are a very helpful man, *Capitán*, for one whose death has been ordered. Shall we kill him now, *compadres*?"

A low titter spread round the circle of men. Slocum didn't see why they had to be so goddamn cheerful about it.

He said, "Just get it over with."

Montoya said, "Whatever you say, *Capitán*." He looked round the circle at his men. They all leveled their guns. "Fire!"

And six *bandidos* fired their pistols into the air.

While Slocum blinked, amazed to find himself still breathing, Montoya said, "You think he is dead enough, *amigos*, or should we kill him some more?"

Manuel, of the Winchester and the blackened eye, opened his mouth. But before he could speak, Montoya said, "I take opinions from everyone except you."

A burly Mexican, the one who had led the black mare to old Pete the day before, fired his gun once more into the air, then holstered it. "Now he is truly dead, I think."

Montoya nodded. "I agree, Hector. Maybe we should pile some rocks, in case the fat one sends men to check, *no*?"

Three of the bandits dismounted and set to work dragging stones to a central point. Montoya leaned on his saddlehorn. "You died well, *Capitán*. You are a brave man."

By this time, Slocum had recovered from the shock of finding himself alive. "Jesus Christ, Montoya!" he snapped. "You could warn a fella!"

"Ah, but my men have so little entertainment." The bandit pointed at Manuel, who was still mounted, and sitting a few yards away, stroking the Winchester. "And now we will have a souvenir to show O'Hara. We will bury the Colts with you, out of respect."

"Gosh, thanks," Slocum said dryly.

Montoya threw him a half-filled water bag, which he tied around his saddlehorn. "There is enough water in your canteens and this to take you and your horse to the first water hole. You know how to find it?"

"With my eyes closed."

"*Bueno*. The passage straight ahead is the one you came in through."

Slocum nodded. "You'll watch out for Yancy?"

"We will do our best."

"Good. You know if anybody else has been sent? With the real telegrams, I mean."

"No. I think it was done in Tucson already, Slocum. I think it is too late."

The *bandidos* had made a passable cairn, and were mounting up again. Montoya said, "Ride swiftly, señor." And with that, the bandits were off the way they came, dust kicking up around their horses' heels until all he could see was the roil.

He started toward the rock passage.

17

Maddie woke from a light doze to the sound of wagons and shouts. She rose and wandered down the hall. As she neared the front of the hacienda, the shouts grew louder. Men on the porch, men on the courtyard, men everywhere. Through the window, she spied Daddy Jim's bald head.

"Spies!" Daddy Jim barked. "There is nothing lower than a sneaking spy. Bring them forward."

What was he up to? Nothing to do with Slocum, she hoped. She crept forward until she could see him—and the wide plaza beyond the porch—clearly.

Guards brought forward three troopers, their hands bound behind them, and shoved them to their knees. They'd already been beaten. Two had bloodied noses, all three were scratched and bruised about the face, and one had a split lip. They were all in Confederate uniforms, now dirty and ripped. Troopers.

She was glad to see Slocum wasn't among them, but the sigh of relief was barely out of her when she heard Daddy Jim say, "I am

ashamed, gentlemen, ashamed to think that
you'd underestimate me so. You have dined
on my larder, had congress with my whores,
and stayed alive in this inhospitable land only
because of my generosity. Well, you have ful-
filled your destinies. The information you've
channeled to your superiors in the outside
world served my purposes, but that time is at
an end. I have no further use for you. General,
execute them. And be quick about it."

What? No trial? And then she realized the
concept of a trial held by these madmen was
ludicrous, that this whole camp, the army, the
officers and the men in it, was more insane
than the darkest fantasy of any client she'd
ever had.

Before, she'd managed to stay above it, even
while she was in the thick of it. She'd seen the
whole thing as some kind of amusing fantasy
that Daddy Jim was playing out with his
friends. Even the knowledge that they planned
to attack Tucson hadn't sunk in, not really, not
completely, until now.

This wasn't just big boys playing games.
These were grown-up men with guns and cannons, and deadly intent.

She sat down at the table, shaking, only to
jump to her feet again when the sound of three
shots, closely spaced, pierced the air. Help-
lessly, she looked out the window. Beyond
Daddy Jim's head, the men lay in the courtyard, face-down in dirt turned to rust by

streaming blood. The troopers behind them holstered their pistols.

"Good," said Daddy Jim. "Spike their heads." The bodies were dragged off.

She collapsed into the chair again. Her stomach had gone quaky and she had a pressing urge to vomit. She willed herself to hold it back, to be strong. She had a feeling things were only going to get worse, but at least she had Slocum. Slocum would fix things, make it all right. He'd at least get her the hell out of here.

One of the officers, Major Somebody-or-other, was suddenly standing over her. "Mrs. Osborn?" he said formally, when she finally thought she could look up at him without spitting in his face. "President O'Hara requires your presence on the porch."

President O'Hara? Somehow, she managed to stand up. *You can do this, Maddie, you can do this.* . . .

She smiled, although her face felt numb, and took the major's arm. On wobbling legs, she went outside.

"Ah, there you are, my little daffodil!" Daddy Jim enthused. "Come witness my hour of glory!"

She stepped behind him, and forced herself to kiss his bald, sweaty head. The courtyard—the whole complex, for that matter—was alive with activity, although she didn't see Slocum anywhere.

A long line of wagons was proceeding out of the canyon, the drivers cracking their whips and shouting at the mules and horses. Men hurried this way and that, carrying supplies, carrying armfuls of rifles or blankets or kegs of powder.

To her right, off by the corrals, several men stood in a cluster. They were chopping at something with a machete.

It took her a second to understand that they were severing the heads from the bodies of the "spies" they had just executed.

Spike them, Daddy Jim had said.

Mad. They were all mad.

Daddy Jim twisted his head to look at her. "What's wrong, my peach?"

She made herself smile, made herself beam. Where was Slocum? "Nothing, Daddy Jim. Would you like a shoulder rub? Or maybe it's too hot for that. Limeade?"

He was about to answer her when the *bandidos* swept through the pass and past the wagons, cut past the officers barracks, and thundered toward the hacienda. Daddy Jim rocked forward in his chair to greet them. She clung to the back of it, holding herself erect. To the side, a soldier picked up a severed head and stuck it under his arm, like a ball.

The *bandidos* stopped, horses rearing in the cloud of dust, and the leader, that disgusting Montoya, doffed his sombrero and said, "*Patrón*, it is done."

Daddy Jim said, "Thought for sure you'd bring that stallion back."

Maddie stiffened.

Montoya shrugged. "He would not be caught, and I did not want to take the time to convince him. But there is no water in that canyon. I think when we go back tomorrow or the next day, he will see reason."

Daddy Jim nodded thoughtfully. "And Slocum is dead?"

Maddie's knees buckled. Only her hands on the back of the rocker held her up.

"Oh *sí*," Montoya said, as if killing Slocum had bored him. "Many bullets. Many holes. He died bravely, though. He did not flinch. We buried him."

Daddy Jim barked, "I thought I told you to leave him for the crows to pick clean!"

Montoya held out one hand, palm up. "Sorry, *Patrón*. We forgot. But Manuel has a new rifle."

Manuel raised the Winchester and yipped loudly, spinning his horse.

Daddy Jim suddenly rocked back, nearly throwing Maddie to the ground, and laughed.

Hanging on to the furniture, she pulled herself over to the chair beside him and sat down. She couldn't smile anymore, couldn't play the game. Slocum was dead. She'd never see him again, never feel him touch her in the dark, never again hear him whisper her name. Never hear him call her a bitch or kiss her or dump her off his horse or slip his hand high between her legs and drive her wild.

"Well done," Daddy Jim was saying, "well done. You boys go give Lieutenant Cosgrove a hand with the artillery then."

He turned toward Maddie, his face suddenly flooded with concern. "My dear, you don't look at all well."

"The heat," she heard herself whisper through numb lips. Every part of her seemed to have gone dead.

"Nonsense," said Daddy Jim. "You just need some food. We all need food." He leaned closer, and it took every last ounce of willpower she had left not to shrink away.

"Don't you worry about these filthy Mexicans, sugar pie," he whispered. "You won't have to put up with them much longer." He twisted toward the open window. "Maria! Some lunch!"

Then something caught his eye. A wagon, she thought, although she didn't have the strength to turn and look.

Staring past her, he clasped his hands together like a child, and beamed, "Oh, my cannons! There go my cannons!"

Slocum made it to the water hole by dusk, and he camped there. He was up before first light, filled the water bag tight as a tick, and was off again.

A few days off the trail had done wonders

for the stud, and he made better time than Slocum had hoped. By late afternoon—when O'Hara's men would just be in sight of the Santa Ritas, according to what he'd been told—he had already passed them on the north, crossed the Santa Cruz River, and was galloping flat out across the parade grounds at Fort Lowell, in Tucson.

Several soldiers shouted at him as he skidded the appy to a stop in front of headquarters. One tried to grab him as he pushed his way into the general's anteroom, and he slugged the trooper in the jaw. The sergeant at the desk was on his feet.

"I've gotta see General Miles right now. It's urgent."

The sergeant, a middle-aged Irish bull who looked due for retirement any day, crossed his arms. "I'll be decidin' how urgent it is, laddie. First off, why don't you start explainin' why you went and hit Corporal O'Flaherty, and him just making a polite inquiry."

Slocum said, "Look, it's imperative I see Miles, you understand? Yancy Tate sent—" He heard a rustle behind him, and turned around just in time to duck. O'Flaherty was up and swinging. He missed, but Slocum didn't, and landed a fist square in his midsection.

It knocked the air out of O'Flaherty's sails, all right, but the big sergeant was on him before he could turn around. A meaty fist landed against his jaw and knocked him back against the wall. He ducked under the left hook that immediately followed, scrambling to the side, and landed a blow to the sergeant's belly that would have doubled over any other man.

The sergeant looked down at Slocum's fist, still hard against his stomach, then looked up and smiled. "Don't you know that you've got to have an appointment, boyo?" he said, and then slugged Slocum in the chin.

Wet, was the first thing that crawled through Slocum's brain. *I'm wet*. And then a torrent of water hit his face. Slocum sat up quickly, sure he was drowning in some crazy dream-river, and Maddie was drowning with him.

"That's enough, Sergeant," someone said as he fell back on the pillow. He was on a cot. They didn't have cots in rivers, he was fairly certain of that.

"Slocum? Slocum! Can you hear me?"

The voice echoed in his skull, but he recognized it. Unfortunately. He pulled himself up on his elbows and shook his head, trying to clear his vision.

General Miles stood over him, and he didn't look pleased. Beside him stood the sergeant. He was grinning, and there was a bucket swinging in his hand.

Slocum swung his legs over the side of the cot and held his head in his hands. "Quite a punch you've got there, Sarge," Slocum said.

"I can hold me own," the sergeant answered happily.

"Rafferty!" barked General Miles.

The sergeant came to attention. "Beggin' your pardon, General, sir."

The general turned to Slocum. "Nice of you to surrender. I take it you wanted to say something before I throw your miserable hide in jail. Where, I might add, you will reside for the rest of your puny, sniveling, worthless life."

Slocum looked up, a few drops of water dripping off the end of his nose. "Now, General, that business was so long ago that I figured you fellas had forgot all about—"

"Take him to the guardhouse, Rafferty."

As Rafferty hauled him to his feet, Slocum said, "Yancy Tate sent me! Look!" He fished in his shirt pocket, and flipped Miles the gold eagle that O'Hara had tossed to him yesterday afternoon.

Rafferty had dragged him halfway to the door before Miles, staring at the coin, said, "Stop."

Slocum breathed a sigh of relief.

Rafferty looked annoyed.

"Leave us," said Miles. His face held no humor whatsoever. "And get me Major Perrini and Captain Meyers, on the double. And see that Slocum's horse is taken care of. I assume you're riding a nice one. Who'd you steal it from?"

As Rafferty closed the door behind him, Slocum wiped his face on his sleeve, then said, "Didn't steal him from anybody. That was all just a little misunderstanding, General, and . . ."

He remembered why he was here. He ran fingers through his hair, combing out water. "Yancy said I was to talk to you alone."

"Perrini and Meyers are all right." Grimly, General Miles sat down behind his desk, turning the small gold coin over and over in his hand. "O'Hara's on the march, isn't he?"

18

Maddie dove under the big dining table, curled into a fetal position, and clapped her hands over her ears. All hell had broken loose in the camp, and for the third time today.

She cringed when a stray bullet splintered the wood about a foot from her face, and she scrambled away from it, still under the table. In the lamplight, she could see men's legs running up the hall, running from window to window, hear their shouts, hear the *ping* of brass casings as they hit the floor.

"Hit that sonofabitch Montoya!" she heard Daddy Jim bellow. "Riddle the Mex bastard with bullets! Make him bleed!"

"But we can't see him! He's too well hid!" came the answer.

"Shoot him anyway!" Daddy Jim thundered.

To the sound of gunfire, she began to crawl, on hands and knees, toward the hall, toward what she felt was the safety of her room. If she could just get to her room, there wouldn't be any noise, she told herself. No cries of pain, no soldiers sprawled, dead and dying, on the floor. No gunfire, no whoops or taunts from outside.

She had crawled almost to the end of the table when she realized that her room was already occupied. What was it? Something about a private. A dead private, the back of his head blown away. Was he propped in her window?

Slocum. She'd go to Slocum's room. He'd know what to do.

But Slocum was dead. She had killed him by bringing him here.

Suddenly, a hand reached beneath the table and yanked her up like a rag doll. Daddy Jim held her up by the back of her dress and gave her a shake.

"Reload," he growled, then dropped her.

A corporal screamed and dropped his gun, backing away from the shuttered window. Blood streamed between the fingers he held over his face. As he fell and another soldier moved into his place, Maddie stepped toward him, only to be pulled back again.

"I said, reload!" Daddy Jim shoved a rifle into her hands and pushed her down into a chair. "Where's that cockroach Montoya?" he demanded. "I want him killed! I want his head!"

With shaking fingers, Maddie managed to reload the rifle and pushed it aside, grabbing another from the pile. The stench of blood filled her nostrils. Blood and hot brass and sweat and kerosene.

The hacienda was like the inside of a black cookstove and had been since morning, when the first shots had rung out, when it had begun. It was afternoon now, the hottest part of the day, but the bars in the windows had been rung down, the shutters had been swung closed—keeping the light out but the heat in—and they were inside what amounted to a gigantic sweatbox.

"Do you see him, Miller?"

Daddy Jim again. She didn't look up, just cracked open another rifle and shoved in the cartridges.

"No, sir."

"DuLac?"

"No, sir, Mr. President."

"Keep your eyes peeled! He's tricky. Goddamned greasy Mexicans! I should have killed them the first . . ."

A scream from outside. Frank had been screaming all day, off and on. Lord knows what they were doing to him down inside the officers barracks.

"Shut up!" Daddy Jim roared, and smacked her across the face, knocking her halfway out of her chair. She didn't realize until he hit her that she'd been moaning: a thin, helpless wail to go with Frank's powerless pleas for help, pleas that had turned into animal sounds by noon, and now were almost unrecognizable.

She righted herself and grabbed another rifle. The two she'd loaded had already been snatched away. Numbly, she began to reload it, not caring that the metal was hot and scorched her fingers, not caring when another stray slug barely missed her lantern and buried itself in the wood of the tabletop.

Frank screamed again.

Suddenly, she pushed away from the table, crying, "Give it to them! Just let them take it! He's your son, Daddy Jim, your only son!"

In the center of the room, drenched with sweat, O'Hara looked up from the groaning corporal he was standing over and said, "I never liked him." He aimed his pistol at the wounded boy's head and pulled the trigger.

Maddie jumped, and would have vomited again if she'd had anything left to throw up. "Just give them the gold!" she sobbed, her vision blurred by tears. "You can get more. For the love of God, you can get more! What's this compared with the lives of these men?"

She swept a trembling hand toward the corner, where sack upon sack of gold dust had been piled next to a tower of bars. "What's this compared to *your* life?"

Just then, she felt her arm burn, felt like someone had shoved her back a step. She looked down to see blood, her own blood, rapidly darkening her sleeve.

Daddy Jim, growing dim, stared at her. "You're shot, Maddie," he said matter-offactly, and it sounded distant and filled with soft echoes. "Take care of it. And get back to work."

Slocum told them everything he knew.

He repeated what Yancy had said and the slightly different plan O'Hara had laid out. Major Perrini had him go over what he'd seen in the encampment three times, particularly the number of cannons and Gatling guns. Early on, Captain Meyers left the room for fifteen minutes, nodding once to General Miles when he returned, taking his chair quietly.

For two hours, Slocum talked. He talked until he was hoarse, and then he talked some more. He heard a racket outside, but since nobody else seemed distracted by it, he just went on talking.

These boys were real particular about knowing exactly how well O'Hara was armed, and exactly with what, and Slocum told them everything he remembered, from the time he arrived in the camp until the time he left. He told them quite a bit he didn't know he remembered too, information he'd picked up out of the corner of his eye without realizing it. Perrini was a good interrogator.

Finally, Miles pushed back his chair. "Ten minutes, gentlemen," he said.

Perrini and Meyers took their leave. Miles looked up from the gloves he was putting on, and said, "Well, what are you waiting for?"

Slocum stood up. "You done with me?"

Miles frowned. "You're about two jumps away from a firing squad. You know that, don't you?"

Slocum ignored the remark. "What about O'Hara's boys in Tucson? And Prescott and Bisbee and the others?"

"Horsefeathers. He's got about twenty in town, which are probably rounded up by now. You heard the commotion. And three that we know of in camp. I've had them arrested too."

"And Prescott?"

"I can't help them now. I sent wires. Well, Meyers sent wires. But I'd be surprised if he has more than fifteen, twenty men up there. Fewer in the other communities. The thing about O'Hara is that his reach has always exceeded his grasp. Frankly, I didn't expect this assault to ever take place. Washington expected him to sit out there and play dictator or king or whatever—"

"President."

"President." Miles shook his head. "Well, they thought he'd never do anything really constructive. Or destructive. Horsefeathers and horseshit, that's all he is. Never thought I'd live to see the day."

He picked up the gold coin Slocum had given him and turned it over in his hand, then looked up. "Hoped I never would. These men. These boys he's got in his 'army.' I'll bet that most of them aren't twenty years old."

Slocum thought on it. Miles was close to right. "A few middle-aged, but mostly they're young."

"Never seen a battle. And they're going to die for something so horrible that they can't imagine it. If you told them O'Hara's plans for the Territory—his *real* plans—half of them would strip off those uniforms, and the other half wouldn't believe you. He's one deluded bastard."

Slocum didn't speak. He agreed with Miles's assessment.

The general picked up his hat and snugged it on his head. "Well, none of those boys are going to die if I have anything to do with it, Slocum. As few of them as possible anyway. I put an end to the Apache Wars. I brought in Geronimo without spilling a single drop of blood."

Slocum had some argument with that—a great deal of argument, as a matter of fact—but kept his mouth shut.

"And if I can do that, I can damn well put down a little insurrection." Miles was ready to ride, all spit and polish and brass buttons. He stared at Slocum. "Well? What are you waiting on? Don't you have to go back for that girl?"

He'd been so busy reciting the numbers of horses and cannons that he'd forgotten he'd told them about Maddie. "Yessir," he said. "I do. But I've got a question for you first.

O'Hara was waiting for a message. What was it?"

Miles shrugged. "Hard to tell. Although we moved out about a dozen . . ." He stopped, frowning. "I don't have to tell you a damned thing."

"Sorry. Just asking."

"Well, get the hell out of here then. As far as I'm concerned you were never here. But don't let me see you again, Slocum."

Slocum started out the door, but Miles called after him. "Tell her that her marriage isn't legal. Turnbull was never a justice of the peace, just Bob Turner, born in Georgia and late of Cedar Rapids, Iowa. A two-bit bartender with delusions of grandeur. And tell her something else."

Slocum's hand was on the latch. He wanted to get out of there before General Miles changed his mind. "What's that?"

"Tell Miss Sewell—or Miss O'Hara or Mrs. Osborn or whatever she's calling herself—that she owns that land O'Hara's been mining. It was her father's. If she has any trouble claiming it, have her wire me."

Suddenly the pieces came together. Maddie babbling at him about Frank, about O'Hara lying about her having consumption.

He said, "I think she already knows."

Miles scowled. "Then what are you waiting for? Get your thieving butt out of here."

Slocum didn't have to be told twice.

Outside, night had fallen. The nearly full moon illuminated the troops mustering on the parade ground in a bluish haze, and his horse was tacked up and waiting for him. He vaulted not into Pete's saddle, but the saddle of the sorrel gelding next to the appy, and leading Pete, lit out at a lope.

He was halfway across the parade ground before he heard Miles shout, "*Slocum!*"

He kicked the gelding in the ribs, passing line upon line of cavalry and artillery, until he was off the parade grounds, clear of Fort Lowell and Tucson, and across the Santa Cruz.

He eased the sorrel down into a jog and looked over at Pete. Two hours rest didn't make up for a day and a half of riding hard, and he figured to make the trip back as easy as possible on him. Slocum would travel until midnight, then camp for three hours, maybe four. He'd make the canyon by the next afternoon.

He reined the sorrel in and reached into his pocket, pulling out his fixings. He rolled himself a quirlie and lit it up, thinking about the horse that General Miles was still mad over. A pretty-headed black-bay, that one, and he sure could run. Slocum had only kept him a week before he sent him back, but General Miles could sure stay mad over a horse for a long time. He was probably going to stay mad over this one too.

He smiled, and reached over to pat Pete's

neck. "Yup. He can hold a grudge near about as long as I can."

She was in Slocum's room, a rag wrapped about her thudding arm, when she regained consciousness. It was dark—truly dark, for no light came through the two gun ports in the shutters—and quiet. She wondered what time it was, then decided it didn't matter. Nothing mattered.

She turned on her side, wincing at her arm, and stroked the blankets beside her. Good old Slocum, lying under a pile of rocks in some godforsaken canyon. The blankets had his scent, the way she'd known him last. Leather. Musk.

She felt hollow inside, as hollow as if she'd been a melon that Daddy Jim had gutted right down to the rind. Why did men do the things they did? Why did anyone do anything?

She rolled onto her back again, for it was easier on her wounded arm, and stared up through the darkness at the ceiling. She wondered if Frank was dead yet. No man deserved to die like that, not even Frank.

A chill took her, despite the heat, and she hugged herself. Daddy Jim had said they were fighting two battles—the one against the Mexicans outside and the one for the Sovereign Republic of New Albion. He had said his troops would be licking General Miles first thing in the morning, and that they'd be back—or at least, a few men would be back to get him, to carry him into Tucson in triumph.

She hoped General Miles flattened his troops. She hoped they smashed them into the ground. And in a way, she hoped the Mexicans finished off Daddy Jim. She'd go down right along with him—she didn't have any choice, did she?—but it would be worth it to rid the world of a rat like him.

A big, fat, crazy, lying, plague-carrying rat.

She'd been a fool. Playing games, that's what she'd been doing, playing games with her life and wasting it. All these years, years when she could have been doing something—making a home and family, or starting a bakery, or even going on the goddamn stage—she'd been playing games. Games with the customers, games with Daddy Jim, games with Slocum.

Well, maybe not with Slocum, not at the end. But she was sorry about all that time on the desert. She wished she could take it all back, start out with him all over again as herself. As Maddie Sewell.

The door opened. Private Du-Somebody stood in the doorway, a lantern in his hand. "Miz Osborn?" he drawled softly. "The President wonders if you could maybe get us together some dinner?"

The President.

Bah.

Well, it wasn't this boy's fault. He looked as

scared as she had felt up until a minute ago.
She sat up and brushed sweat-dampened hair
back from her brow. Maria had gone, of
course. She and Pablito had slipped out during
the confusion, while the last troops were pa-
rading out of the canyon, and the last of the
gold was being carried from the "bank" and
up to the house. She was probably down there
right now, whipping up a steer on a spit for
those murdering *bandidos*.

"Miz Osborn?" the trooper said again.

Du-Something. DuLac. That was his name.

"I'll be right there, Private DuLac."

"Yes, ma'am." He turned to leave.

She stopped him. "Wait a minute, Private.
Don't call me . . ." She softened her tone, remembering that they shared the same ultimate
fate. "I mean, please don't call me Mrs. Osborn. My name's Sewell. Miss Sewell."

Funny how you only knew who you were,
who you really were, when you were about to
die.

He gave her a curious look, but said,
"Yes'm," and left.

Slowly, she got to her feet and started down
the dark hallway. She knew the kitchen was
well stocked and the water tanks were full.
Out of twenty soldiers who'd been assigned to
stay behind at headquarters with Daddy Jim,
sixteen were still alive, and they had plenty of
ammunition. She didn't know how many *bandidos* were outside, but she knew there were at

least six, unless others had joined them. More would come later, she knew, from the far canyons.

Maria might be serving up a barbecued steer for the bandits, but there'd be no fresh meat or fresh produce for those inside the hacienda. Beans, rice, and tortillas, she thought as she started down the hall, holding her bad arm with her good.

No more gourmet meals for Daddy Jim. No, no more chocolate mousse or filet mignon, no more eight-egg mushroom omelets or crown roasts. They'd even finished off the last of the fancy canned goods for the wedding celebration. Just beans, beans, and more beans until they were all dead. If not from the bullets, then from the gas. Farted to death in a closed house in summer in Arizona. Good Lord!

She clamped a hand over her mouth, holding in the laughter that had been born of hysteria, but she was still grinning as she entered the great room and walked through it, past a snoozing Daddy Jim, past the pile of gold and the pile of dead troopers' ripening bodies, past the long shadows of men peering out into the darkness, into their own deaths.

She went into the kitchen and, humming a macabre tune, began to dig out the pots and pans.

19

Slocum slept longer than he planned, and he woke to the sound of cannons. Two cannons, to be precise.

He'd camped due north of the western slope of the Santa Ritas, due north of the site where O'Hara had planned to gather his troops for the attack.

It sounded as if Miles had forced the issue.

On the eastern horizon, the sky was streaked with the first pinks and yellows of dawn, and overhead, the stars were disappearing. To the south, one more cannon fired, its blast sounding as thin and distant—but as unmistakable—as the first two.

And then nothing.

Slowly, Slocum stood, letting his body wake up at its own pace. He watched the southern horizon for a time, expecting to see the glow of torches and the smoke from guns and the faraway reports of rifles. He expected, at least, to hear the distant roar of troops, sounding a battle cry as they charged with bayonets. An army that big made a sound that carried.

But again, there was nothing. He fed the

horses as he chewed a chunk of jerky, wondering all the while what the hell was going on down there. And he wondered, as he tightened the last girth and swung up on the sorrel, if it was possible. Had Miles put down this "little insurrection," as he called it, so easily?

He was sorely tempted to swing south and have a look-see for himself, but the fact that Maddie was waiting for him—and more importantly, the fact that he'd discovered, belatedly, that it was Miles's own mount he'd made off with—put a decided damper on the inclination.

He clucked to Pete, squeezed the sorrel between his legs, and was off, headed west for Los Cuervos.

Maddie was in the kitchen again.

Although it was noon and blindingly bright outside, it was dark inside the hacienda. The only illumination came from the lanterns and the tiny shafts of dust-mote-filled light that came through the gun ports. Besides being dark, it was unbearably hot and fetid.

They'd opened the door for a minute before dawn—just long enough to throw the bloating bodies out on the porch—but what little air had come in had long since vanished, and the stench of the bodies remained.

She had given up on ever being dry again. Sweat soaked every inch of her clothing, ran down her throat and between her breasts. The sodden waistband of her skirt clung to her waist like a wet snake.

The oven didn't help matters. It was twenty degrees hotter here than in the rest of the house, and that had to be one hundred and fifteen. She would have given anything for a nice, lukewarm beer. It would have tasted like ice to her, like heaven.

Everything was going bad. The milk had gone over during the night, and sat curdling in a corner. She'd cooked the last of the meat the evening before, in three huge pans of enchiladas that the men were still eating—those that had any appetite left anyway.

She wasn't sure about the eggs, but she was going to use them up. Something special, just for Daddy Jim. She cracked them into the sugar, the vanilla, and the last of the pooled butter. Good. The whites were cooked, just a little around the edge of the shells, but that was all. He'd never notice.

She began to beat them together with the sugar mixture, sweat dripping from her face into the bowl. She cursed softly that the melted butter didn't have the right consistency for creaming, but kept on beating it with a big wooden spoon as she walked slowly back and forth to create a breeze.

It was quiet now, just an occasional shot. Mercifully, Frank hadn't screamed all day. She hoped he was dead.

The *bandidos*, it seemed, had decided to

starve them out. They'd tried burning them out at around three in the morning, throwing torches in the windows and up on the roof, but the hacienda wouldn't catch. The only casualty had been a scorched shutter that Daddy Jim's men hadn't found right away.

All the men were nerved up, Daddy Jim among them, though she thought she was the only one to know it. He sat in his chair, stinking and soaking wet and bright pink, and fanning his chins and belly with a lady's fan of black Spanish lace.

He'd been down to his underwear by ten in the morning. They all had been, at least, down to their skivvy tops. She'd stripped down to a camisole and skirt, and would have gotten rid of the pantalets too, except that they kept her legs from chafing.

About an hour ago, just before she'd decided to make something special for Daddy Jim, she'd been out in the dining hall when Private DuLac had made his plea.

"Mr. President, sir?" he'd said, coming up out of the corner in his sweat-soaked undershirt, with his hair plastered to his head. "I respectfully submit, that is, I mean . . ."

Daddy Jim had paused in his fanning. "Out with it, boy!" he'd barked.

Sweat had run down DuLac's face, dripped off the end of his nose. "Well, it's just . . . I think we oughta throw the gold out." A few of the men had murmured their approval. Bolstered, DuLac had continued. "I mean, it's better than us bakin' alive in here, sir. I think we—"

She'd never heard the rest of what Private DuLac thought, because Daddy Jim had picked up his pistol and shot a gaping hole in Private DuLac's chest.

DuLac had just stood there for a moment, mouth open and moving but no sound coming out.

Daddy Jim, disgusted, had looked at him and said, "Oh, for God's sake, fall down."

He had. He'd been dead before he hit the floor.

"Never should have trusted the goddamned froggy French," Daddy Jim had said, and then had looked up, into the stunned faces of the others. "Well? Anybody else want to give our treasury to a band of simpleminded cutthroats? Anybody else want to give up, when our men will be returning in victory any minute?"

No one had said a word.

And Maddie had decided to bake something special.

She measured the flour and the salt and the soda and set them to one side. She poured shelled pecans into a marble mortar and ground them coarsely, then dumped them into a separate bowl.

Then she chose a glass from the cupboard, and broke it on the tiled countertop.

"Maddie?" came Daddy Jim's voice. "Are you all right, sweet pea?"

As long as she was in the kitchen, she was his sweet pea.

"Yes, Daddy," she called, carefully sorting through the sharp shards, looking for the thinnest ones. "I just broke a glass, that's all."

"All right, sugar pie. What are you doing?"

"Making something special," she answered, gingerly putting four long tongues of glass into the mortar. "Something sweet. Something just for you, Daddy Jim."

Under her breath, she added, "It's from Slocum. And Private DuLac."

Humming, she began to grind the glass.

Slocum made his way along the zigzagging path, high above the canyon floor. He was riding the appaloosa now, and leading Miles's sorrel, and hoping the sorrel wouldn't take a bad step. If he did, Slocum was prepared to drop the lead rope and keep on moving. The sorrel was a nice horse for an army mount, but not nice enough to take a chance on sending Pete—or himself—over the edge.

But the sorrel followed Pete along carefully, picking his footing with care, and finally they slid down the slope next to the entrance to O'Hara's canyon.

He sat quietly for a moment. The canyon he was in was wide and long and dry, and the trampled sagebrush and cholla showed that great many wagons and men had recently gone through. All of them out, none of them in, which was a good sign. It meant that no riders had come from the battle. O'Hara was still cut off, without communication.

No sound came from the canyon beyond. He imagined O'Hara had stayed behind— President Lincoln hadn't ridden into battle, and neither had Jeff Davis, so why should O'Hara be any different? O'Hara would have kept a few men with him—to guard the gold if nothing else—and he would have kept Maddie.

O'Hara could keep the men. It was Maddie and the gold he was interested in. The question was, how did a man, a man who was supposed to be dead, ride in there?

He got down off Pete, slid one Colt from its holster, and started forward, leading the horses.

The place where the two canyons joined was a narrower passage, about twenty feet wide with the walls soaring up and in. They didn't meet at the top, but there was a decent overhang. Slocum kept to the side, watching the rims overhead for the shadows of any guards O'Hara had posted, and the dust below for signs of any tracks going in.

He found neither, but he was still wary. Fifty yards later, he walked forward and crouched in the roiled dust and manure left by the passing of a couple of hundred horses. He surveyed the camp.

It was quiet. No guards, which was odd, and not a soul was outside, with the exception of a dead horse, bloating out past the barracks and covered with arguing crows. The flag was different. The Confederate banner was gone, and in its place flew a white flag, a white flag with some kind of green and blue emblem in the center.

Slocum filled his cheeks with air, then blew it out through his teeth with a hiss. The crazy sonofabitch. Of course he had a flag. Didn't he have an army? No guards, but an army.

Then, for the first time, he dropped his gaze to the hacienda. Bodies littered the porch and the courtyard. Slocum winced at the surprise of it. The ground was speckled with crows: those fighting amongst themselves over the corpses, and those who were feasting.

He couldn't be sure how many dead men were outside. At least four. Maybe five or six. He was fairly certain Maddie wasn't among them, though. Daddy Jim O'Hara wasn't, that was for certain. He could have spotted O'Hara mountainous corpse a quarter mile off.

A crow took wing, and Slocum's gaze followed it. It landed on a tall pole, and began pecking the round thing at its top. It took him a second to recognize just what the crow was pecking at, what it was stripping the flesh off.

Slocum stood up and looked away from the

severed heads, swallowing back the vomit, thinking about Yancy, and trying *not* to think about him.

Right now, he had to think straight.

Somebody had been shooting, that was certain, and from this side of the hacienda. The only place to give sufficient shelter was the officers barracks. So he had two choices: He could go there, or the big house.

Either camp was just as prone to be the wrong one. The house would have O'Hara, who'd likely shoot him—or worse—on sight. The barracks might be full of renegade Apaches up from Mexico, for all he knew. Or they might be empty. Or they might contain Montoya and his men. He hoped it was Montoya. Either way, the barracks had, at least, the advantage of being closer.

Slocum decided to take his chances on the barracks. He holstered his gun and brought up the appy and the sorrel, close together, side by side. Then he stepped between them, and got one foot in the stud's off stirrup.

"You see that building down there?" he said under his breath, indicating the officers barracks, and past it, the dead horse. "We're gonna go just as fast as we can to the back of it. Now, don't foul this up, or you're gonna end up like your late cousin out there."

It didn't do any good to talk to the horses, he figured, but it didn't hurt anything either.

He took a grip on the reins and the saddle-horns, and then, hoisting himself up between the bodies of the two mounts, cried, *"Yaaa!"*

The sorrel jumped a little ahead of Pete, and for a second Slocum was afraid he'd be torn in two, but then the animals started moving in unison. He would have congratulated himself had there been time, and if the horses hadn't begun to veer apart as quickly as they had moved together.

To make matters worse, somebody was firing. He let go of Pete and clung to the sorrel for three more strides. It was enough to carry him to the backside of the barracks, where he dropped to the ground. The horses kept running, headed for the paddocks.

He was alive. For the moment anyway.

Whoever had been shooting at him had stopped. He pulled both Colts, flattened himself against the rough adobe wall of the building, and began to inch toward the corner. He was about to peer around it when a voice said, "You know, *Señor Capitán,* you are no so tough an *hombre*. My men could have picked you off easy, you lingered in the passage so long. Like shooting the turkey."

Slocum let his breath out. Montoya. "Why didn't you shoot, you old bean-eater?" He rounded the corner, holstering his Colts.

As they walked down the length of the building, Montoya grinned, showing off the gap where his eyetooth should have been. "Well, maybe it was not so easy. But my men were tempted. Manuel has taken such a liking to that Winchester that I think any day he will propose marriage. I let him shoot toward the hacienda instead."

They came to the door, and Montoya said, "I would advise you to go in low. There is only one window at this end of the barracks, and O'Hara's men, they take pleasure in shooting at it."

Montoya fired one round toward the house, more to scare the crows than anything else, Slocum figured, for it popped dirt about ten feet from the porch, and the birds rose up in a nervous flutter. Then, crouching, the two men hurried past the window and into the dim recesses of the barracks.

20

"Slocum?" The voice came from a bunk in the shadows.

He went to it. "Yancy," he said.

Yancy, bruised and scraped, smiled at him weakly. "You made it back, you old snappin' turtle."

"Yup, I did." Yancy didn't look a bit good, but Slocum didn't let his face give him away. He grinned big and said, "Brought Miles' gelding back with me just to prove it. Where are you shot, partner?"

"In the hip. Reckon that slug's buried in my guts somewhere," he said, the words coming slowly. "Miles' boys better get here quick. Fix me up or put me out of my misery. I just—" Yancy's face went white, and then his eyes closed.

"Yancy!" Slocum bent to him, putting his ear to the man's chest, but Montoya pulled him back.

"Passed out," he said, drawing Slocum away. "He is very bad. Maria sees to him."

He tipped his head toward the corner, where Maria prepared a fresh bandage. The boy, Pablito, sat at her feet. "He was in the far canyon when O'Hara's men rounded up his *compadres*," Montoya went on. "Perhaps you saw their heads, on the sticks?"

Slocum nodded, feeling the sickness rise up again.

"They shot him and saw him fall, but there were a great many horses and they were in a hurry. They left him." Montoya's brow furrowed beneath the brim of his sombrero. "He crawled free of them, but I think the horses stepped on him very much before we found him." He stabbed a thumb over his shoulder. "And, of course, you are acquainted with Frank?"

Colonel Frank Osborn, C.S.A. Reformed, the bridegroom and heir apparent, sat tied to a straight-backed chair in sparkling Confederate majesty: bound, gagged, and drooling. His jacket had been removed and his sleeves rolled up. Flies clustered on the scabby cuts of knife slashes that lined his forearms.

Slocum looked at the man, whose eyes seemed unable to hold a focus, and said, "What happened?"

Manuel leaned forward, from a group in the shadows. "We try to make him scream." He circled a finger at his temple. "He likes it."

Montoya nodded. "Before very long, Juanito has to scream for him." He indicated another of the group. "Say something, Juanito."

The man moved his mouth, but nothing but

a hoarse, undecipherable whisper came out. He held up his hands, smiled, and shrugged.

"You see?" said Montoya. "He screamed very well while his voice held out, though. Better than this loco piece of cow dung."

He kicked Frank's chair, and behind the gag, Frank giggled.

Slocum suddenly remembered the coffeepot, that first night when Frank had ridden into his and Maddie's camp. Frank had picked it up barehanded. It made a sort of lopsided sense now—if any of this made sense, that is.

Montoya sat down at a table near a side window, one of the long row that faced away from the hacienda, and Slocum joined him. "Your return presents a problem, *Capitán*," Montoya began, pouring warm *cerveza* from a pitcher into two clay mugs.

Slocum picked up his beer. "*Gracias*, Carlos." He took a swallow. It was amazing how good warm beer could taste. He set the mug down and fished in his pocket for his papers and tobacco. He was almost out. "What kind of a problem?"

"If you are back, this means that you have been already to Fort Lowell. If you have been to Fort Lowell, this means that you have told General Miles about our fat friend's plan, and he has ridden out to engage the enemy."

Frank giggled again, but both men ignored him.

Slocum gave a final lick to the quirlie and

stuck it in his mouth, then reached for a lucifer. Striking it, he said, "So, what's your problem?"

"The gold, *Capitán*! The cavalry cannot be
far behind you. One day, maybe, if the fat
one's men do not put up much of a fight. And
I do not think they will. Drilling in the desert
is not the same as facing a man who is going
to shoot back." Montoya shook his head
slowly. "I do not think one day is long enough
to starve them out."

"The gold?" Slocum took a long drag on his
quirlie. "It's down at that warehouse. You
showed it to me yourself."

"No longer, señor. The fat one holds it in
his arms. With more men, I could take them.
But the men from the far canyons will not ar-
rive until tonight. And in the morning? Who
knows what will happen?"

"Oh," said Slocum, and tried not to look
happy. He might get his fifteen hundred out
of this yet.

"Carlos?" The *bandido* at the far end of the
barracks, the one who watched the hacienda
from the tiny broken-out window, signaled to
Montoya. "Carlos, I think something is happening."

"What is it, Paco?" Montoya, Slocum close
behind, went to join Paco at end of the building. Crouching low, they listened.

Screams. The screams of a man, growing
louder, seeped, then surged, out of the haci-

enda, punctuated by the crashes of furniture.

Montoya looked at Slocum. Slocum looked at Montoya, and said, "What the hell?"

Behind them, behind his gag, Frank began to laugh.

From behind, Maddie threw her arms around Daddy Jim's neck and hung on. He had crashed through two chairs, splintering one and knocking the other across the room, and his screams split her ears.

"Get him down! Get him down!" she shouted to the troopers. "Daddy Jim! What's wrong?"

As if she didn't know. As if she hadn't sat across from him and smiled and watched him eat, and said, "Just for you, Daddy, my special vanilla pecan cake. Only for you."

She hadn't realized it would be like this.

A trooper caught his arm, then one grabbed hold of his leg, and took a knee to the chest for his trouble. Three more piled on, and they got him into a chair.

Maddie came around the front and tried to calm him—"Daddy Jim, please!"—but he wasn't having any of it. He was still holding his belly, still screaming. He gave an explosive, strangled cough, and it sprayed blood out across the room, over the surprised troopers, over Maddie's sodden camisole, and across her face.

"He's eating me! He's eating me on the inside!'' he cried, blood oozing from his mouth.

He bellowed again, a mindless scream of agony, then threw off the troopers with one huge spasmic effort, picked up a gun, and headed for the door, screaming, ''It's the devil! The devil's ripping my guts!''

''Mr. President! No!'' cried a trooper.

Daddy Jim's hand was on the latch.

''Don't go out there!'' called another.

''Aw, leave him be,'' said a third.

Daddy Jim turned and fired the gun twice, not caring who or what he hit—although he hit the private standing next to Maddie—then lurched out the door.

The air came like a cold wave over Maddie. For a second, she closed her eyes, unable to do anything about the dying boy beside her, unable to halt Daddy Jim because of that wave of fresh, cool air, air that at a hundred degrees seemed frigid, seemed to block out the pain in her arm, seemed to block out all pain.

She heard herself let out an audible sigh, an ''Ah!'' of pure delight, and then the boy who Daddy Jim had shot clutched at her skirts.

Brought back to reality, she frantically pulled at his hands, thinking to arm herself, thinking that when the *bandidos* killed Daddy Jim they'd come for her, thinking that the *bandidos* would only make it official, for she had killed Daddy Jim.

She freed the dying boy's hands from the fabric of her skirts, then took his pistol. ''I'm sorry," she whispered to him, over Daddy Jim's crazed bellows, as the boy died.

She hadn't even known his name.

"I'm sorry," she said to his corpse.

"*Cristo!* It is O'Hara!" Montoya stood up straight, and Slocum was right behind him.

The *bandido* guarding the window smiled, and leveled his rifle at the screaming madman in the courtyard, the madman who fired into the air over and over, and kept pulling the trigger to empty *clicks*. Montoya put a hand on the guard's shoulder. "Wait, Paco."

Behind them, Frank was laughing. The sound was macabre, eerie, especially coming from Frank when his father was dying outside the window.

"Do something about that," Slocum growled, and Manuel, who had left his bunk to investigate the ruckus outside, cracked Frank over the head with the Winchester's butt as he passed him.

"Thanks," mumbled Slocum.

"*Por nada,*" Manuel said as he joined them at the window. "What you think is wrong with him?" he asked.

Outside, O'Hara was spinning in circles, just waving the gun now, crying out in agony. Blood gushed from his mouth.

"Beats me," said Slocum, scratching his head. "Beats me why he don't fall down. He's losin' a lot of blood."

"Maybe he is poisoned?" said Montoya.

"Maybe someone has fed him the ground-up glass," offered Paco, the window guard. "I saw a man who ate it once. He was much like this one."

At the same time, both Slocum and Montoya said, "No."

Paco shrugged.

O'Hara gave a gut-wrenching shriek, then dropped to his knees. The wide front of his sodden underwear was covered in blood. He belched one last bubble of it, thick and dark red, then fell forward.

"*Señor Capitán*, you think he is dead?" Montoya asked.

"I doubt it," Slocum said. "But he's not gonna be doing any more shooting. What we've got to worry about is the fellas in the house."

The door was open, although he couldn't see anyone. He called, "Hello the house! Come out with your hands empty and in the air! Nobody will shoot!"

The guard grinned and set an eye to his sights, but Montoya said, "Paco, wait."

The guard heaved a sigh, grumbled under his breath, and put down his rifle.

From the hacienda, someone yelled, "How do we know that? How do we know them bandits ain't gonna pick us off whilst we're comin' out?"

Then Maddie's voice. "Slocum? Slocum, is that you?"

Suddenly she rushed out the door, blinking in the light. She was down to her camisole and it, along with her face, was stained with a spray of blood. A rag was tied around her upper arm, also bloodstained, and her hair was matted to her head with sweat.

"Slocum?" she cried again, weakly, and fell to her knees at the edge of the porch.

"It's me, Maddie," he answered, as behind her the men began to emerge, some with their hands up, some with them clasped over their heads.

Slocum left the barracks and loped across the dusty courtyard toward her, the *bandidos* following. "Maddie?" he said softly when he reached her, kneeling. All around, O'Hara's soldiers were being tied, hand to hand. "Maddie, are you hurt?"

She looked up at him, her face streaked with sweat and grime and blood, as well as what looked like flour. Her voice thick, she said, "Of course I'm hurt," she said. "What does it look like." Then, "You sonofabitch. I thought you were dead."

She went to slug him, but he was ready for it and turned his head at the last moment. "Asshole," she said, and then she fainted.

Slocum picked her up in his arms, and was just turning into the house when a single shot rang out. He whirled to find Carlos Montoya standing over O'Hara, holstering his pistol. He looked up at Slocum. "I think that after all Paco is right. I think it is ground glass. He would have taken the long time to die."

One of the soldiers twisted against his ropes and glared at Maddie. "Her!" he said. "It was her and that damn cake! She done it!"

Slocum hugged Maddie's unconscious form to him and walked into the house. It was like walking into a blast furnace.

"Good girl," he whispered, as he went back through the heat, toward his bedroom. "Good for you."

21

After he deposited Maddie in his room and threw open the window, threw open all the windows in the rooms up and down along the hall, he went out front again. The *bandidos* were already at work, loading the gold into a wagon.

Slocum watched them for a minute, then said, "What'd you do with O'Hara's men?"

Montoya, who was supervising, leaned back in his chair and said, "They are in the barracks." He stuck his thumb back over his shoulder, indicating one of the buildings behind the hacienda rather than the officers quarters. "Don't worry, *Capitán*. They cannot escape. My men have jammed the bars in the windows and barricaded the door."

"And Yancy?"

"They bring him to the hacienda." He pointed out the window, toward three men who were carefully carrying Yancy, cot and all, toward the house, like some Oriental potentate. "He is not so good. I think maybe he dies before morning."

Slocum shook his head. "Yancy's tougher than that. He'll make it."

Montoya shrugged.

"And Frank?"

Just then the cot, Yancy aboard, came through the door and nearly collided with a bandit laden with gold. Montoya swore at the bandit in Spanish, then helped him pick up the sacks he'd dropped while Yancy's cot came into the house.

Slocum checked him. He was still out cold. Slocum led the men to O'Hara's room and saw that Yancy was transferred to the bed with as few bumps as possible, and then he stood there a moment after they'd gone, looking about him at O'Hara's bedroom.

A madman's lair. What was troubling was that it didn't look that different from any of the other rooms. You'd think there would be a sign, he thought, that the walls would change colors or something. But the only thing out of order was the flag on the wall, the same as the one that was flying atop the hacienda. White, with a blue and green globe in the center and a one word-legend underneath.

Purity.

With one fist, Slocum ripped it from the wall and cast it down to the tiles. He ground it underfoot it on his way out the door.

The Mexicans were loaded up and leaving. All that was left of the store of gold was a few flakes of dust that had escaped the bags, leav-

ing a softly glittering icing on the dirty tile
floor.

All that gold—his gold—Maddie's gold—
going south in a hurry, and there wasn't a
damn thing he could do about it.

He went out front. The crows were, for the
moment, at bay, but he tried not to look at the
bodies upon which they'd been feeding. The
wagons were loaded, and Maria sat in one of
them, in Daddy Jim O'Hara's rocker, sur-
rounded by gold bars, Pablito on the seat next
to her. There'd be no more cooking for crazy
gringos for her. Maybe she could hire her own
crazy gringo to labor in *her* kitchen.

Slocum checked to make sure they hadn't
hitched his horses to the wagons. They'd har-
nessed Maddie's mare, but thankfully neither
of his, and he reminded himself it would be
pushing it to say anything. The appy and the
general's sorrel were down in the corrals,
stripped of their tack, which was draped over
the far side of the fence. Pete gazed forlornly
at the other horses, whickering softly and tossing his mane.

Montoya, crosswise on the wagon seat,
threw something at him. He caught it on reflex, stared at it, then looked up at Montoya.

"I don't mean to question your generosity,
but why?"

The *bandido* chieftain lifted his hands, palms
up. "Why not? Call it honor among thieves, if
you wish. And speaking of honor..." He

twisted on the wagon seat. "Ah, Miguelito! Have you forgotten something?"

Miguel sat his horse about twenty yards out, not moving.

"Miguel!"

Slowly, the *bandido* rode his horse to within fifteen feet of Slocum, stopped, and with a grunt, heaved the Winchester into the air. Slocum caught it, high and one-handed, and gravely said, *"Gracias, Miguel."*

The bandit snorted and wheeled his horse away, galloping after the other wagon, which was already making its way toward the southern entrance to the canyon.

Montoya watched after him, shaking his head. "He was very fond of that rifle, *Capitán.*"

Slocum said, "He can buy the factory. Where's Frank?"

Montoya turned toward him again. One hand gave his mustache a slow stroke. "He is still at the barracks, but I do not think you wish to visit him. He would not make such good conversation. It seems that the Winchester, she has a very hard stock." He shook his head. "Very hard indeed. Of what kind of wood is it made?"

"Carlos. What happened to Frank?"

"Miguel hit him with a little too much gusto, I think."

Slocum watched until the Mexicans were out of the valley before he went inside to the kitchen. He found the spigot for the water tank, then ran two buckets full. On his way down the hall, he stopped to check on Yancy, who was still unconscious. Then, lifting the buckets once more, he went to Maddie.

"So, who cleaned me up?" Maddie asked as she sprawled, naked except for the clean bandage on her arm, on his bed in the lamplight.

"I did," said Slocum. He was leaning back against the headboard, fingers locked behind his neck, watching her. It was a nice view.

Maddie arched a brow and smiled. "Every little nook and cranny?"

"Every one. Come here."

"Just wait a minute. You mean you took off all my clothes and washed me?"

"Yup."

"Here?" She pointed.

He gave a nod.

"And here?" She pointed again.

"Maddie . . ."

"Even *here*?"

Grinning, he made a grab for her. "Especially there," he growled good-naturedly against her ear. Her breasts felt good, pillowed against his chest. All of her felt good.

She chuckled. "Why, Captain Slocum! I do believe you're getting frisky again. And for the third time! What will people think?"

He pulled her tighter against him. "People ought to mind their own business." He slipped a hand between her legs. She was wet again.

"Not so fast, Slocum." She clamped her legs together, catching his hand. "Why'd you give me that gold?"

He shrugged, and thought about tugging his hand free. He decided against it. "Figured they made off with the rest of it," he said. "You might as well have what they left. After all, you don't know if there's anything left in the ground. And I guess I don't need it. Now, if we were to be discussing what I *really* need . . ."

She opened her legs again, nipping at his ear. "Tell me all about it, Slocum," she whispered throatily, squirming against his busy fingers. She let out a little sigh and closed her eyes before she leaned closer and whispered something in his ear.

He nipped her shoulder and grinned lazily, easing two fingers inside her. "Thought I told you not to say that word."

"I wouldn't have to say it if you'd—" She stopped, grinding her hips back into his hand and letting out a little gasp of pleasure. "If you'd just *do* it."

He eased her over onto her back, and settled himself between her legs. "Yes, ma'am," he said, just before he buried himself in her. "Anything you say, ma'am."

• • •

Before dawn, Slocum had already grained and watered the horses, and given them both a good currying. He'd also taken a bucket of water and a cold breakfast of jerky down to the men locked in the barracks, and then tacked up Pete and led him to the hacienda, tying him to the porch rail. He went into the house to check on Yancy one last time, and found Maddie, in a fresh blouse and skirt, at Yancy's bedside.

"How is he?" he asked softly.

"Sleeping." She stood up, and quietly came out into the hall, closing the door behind her. "It's not as bad as you told me," she scolded. "The bullet went right through his hip. Maybe chipped the bone, but that's all. Didn't anyone *look* at it? Well, I checked. I think he's more sore from being stomped on than anything else." She started to move down the hallway, and Slocum followed her. "He won't be moving for a while, that's for sure."

Suddenly, she stopped and turned toward him. "Slocum, do you have to go?"

"Miles and his troopers are going to be here any time," Slocum said gently. "You know that, Maddie." They started walking again, through the shadows to the dim dining hall. "Tell him I fed his damn horse, will you?"

She nodded. He couldn't see her face well enough to read it.

They moved outside. Morning was coming, bringing with it the dawn breeze. The air was still night-cool. The scavenger birds weren't yet awake, still perched in silent black rows along the cliffs of the canyon walls and the roofs of the buildings.

He tilted his head toward the bodies, dark hummocks scattered over the porch, mercifully shadowed. O'Hara's was like a small black mountain, all alone in the center of the courtyard. "Sorry I didn't . . . I mean, there just wasn't time to—"

She pressed her fingers to his lips. "I'll cover them. Cheat the birds a little anyway. Now get going," she said, the dawn breaking.

"Maddie, I—"

"I know." Then she smiled, crookedly. "Maybe I'll see you around sometime. If you're ever up around Three Wives . . ."

"I'll drop in."

She laid a finger along his cheek. "Do."

He gave her one last kiss, and then he stepped up on Pete.

"Good-bye, Slocum." She stepped back up on the porch and stood, feet apart, arms crossed over her chest. "Well? What are you waiting for, you big dumb sonofabitch?" she said with a sudden laugh. "Get out of here!"

He didn't know why he'd worried. Maddie would be fine. He doffed his hat and gave her a grin, then turned and cantered away, toward the canyon's mouth.

●　●　●

A week and a day later, Slocum was eased back in a bath of cool water in the back room of the Great Western's place in Yuma, smoking a cigar and reading the Tucson paper. Sarah Bowman, the Great Western herself, walked in carrying a towel, which she threw at him before she sat down.

"You been lookin' through the dang papers like you half expected to find Jesus Christ himself in there, Slocum."

He plucked the sopping towel out of his bathwater and tossed it aside. "Man's got to keep up on current events, Sarah." He turned the page.

"Well, it makes me nervous, a big handsome buck like you spendin' all his time readin'." She gave a push to her red hair, piled high on her head in curls. "Makes me feel like my girls ain't catchin' your attention."

"Oh, they've got my attention, all right. It's just . . ."

There, on the bottom of page six, was a story. It seemed General Miles had taken his troops out for maneuvers. They were gone five days, and upon their return, the general reported that his men had performed "adequately."

"Just what?" said the Great Western.

He turned the page, but it was all recipes and ladies' concerns.

"Nothing."

With a sigh, she stood up, all six feet of her.

"Well, I'm gonna send Consuelo in here and see if she can get your mind off that paper. I don't seem to be doin' the job."

Slocum heard her leave, but didn't look. He turned back to the story.

That was all there was. No mention of O'Hara, no mention of the two hundred troops, the horses, the artillery, or New Albion. No mention of Maddie. There was a small article, however, at the corner of the page. It seemed that communications to and from the towns of Bisbee and Prescott had been severed for a short time the prior Friday week, but the trouble was soon remedied.

Slocum tossed the paper to one side, shaking his head. They had hushed it all up, every single solitary word of it. Probably disarmed most of those boys and sent them on their way, and stuck the "officers" on a freight train in the middle of the night, bound for detention and questioning somewhere back East.

He reached toward the little table that held his personal items, and opened his tobacco pouch. He felt around in it, and pulled out a coin, shaking it loose from the tobacco. He'd seen it glowing softly on the floor of the dining hall the morning he'd left Maddie. The *bandidos* had missed it.

It looked, on first glance, like a gold eagle. Same size, same weight. Newly minted, and not a scratch on it. But it was exactly like the coin O'Hara had tossed to him, the same coin that he'd tossed to General Miles the next day. On one side was stamped a globe, with the words "New Albion" boldly standing out at the top and the legend "Purity" at the bottom. On the reverse, the coin held a portrait of a fat, bald man in profile. At the top was engraved, "One Land, One Race." At the bottom, it said simply, "O'Hara the First."

Maybe he'd ride up north, after a few days, up Three Wives way. Just to make sure she was all right, that was all.

Slim brown hands slid over his shoulders, down his chest. In his ear, a voice whispered, "Sarah says you are lonely, my big strong cowboy." The hands slid lower and his cock leapt to life. "You want to come look at my mirrors again, *mi corazón*?"

He flipped the coin into the air with his thumb, and heard it land on the tabletop even as he drew Consuelo around the side of the tub. As she smiled, doe-eyed, he eased her loose top away, exposing lush brown breasts tipped with the color of dark cinnamon.

"Right here is just fine, darlin'," he said, pulling free the cord that tied her skirt and pulling her, naked and laughing, into the tub.